WANTED:
PERFECT PARTNER

WANTED:
PERFECT PARTNER

DEBBIE MACOMBER

THORNDIKE
CHIVERS

This Large Print edition is published by Thorndike Press, Waterville, Maine, USA and by AudioGO Ltd, Bath, England.
Thorndike Press, a part of Gale, Cengage Learning.

The text of this Large Print edition is unabridged.
Other aspects of the book may vary from the original edition.
Set in 16 pt. Plantin.

LIBRARY OF CONGRESS CATALOGING-IN-PUBLICATION DATA

Macomber, Debbie.
    Wanted : perfect partner / by Debbie Macomber. — Large print ed.
        p. cm. — (Thorndike Press large print romance)
    ISBN-13: 978-1-4104-2909-4
    ISBN-10: 1-4104-2909-1
    1. Single mothers—Fiction. 2. Mothers and daughters—Fiction. 3. Personals—Fiction. 4. Large type books. I. Title.
    PS3563.A2364W36 2010
    813'.54—dc22   2010036529

BRITISH LIBRARY CATALOGUING-IN-PUBLICATION DATA AVAILABLE

Published in 2010 in the U.S. by arrangement with Harlequin Books S.A.
Published in 2011 in the U.K. by arrangement with Harlequin Enterprises II B.V.

U.K. Hardcover: 978 1 408 49395 3 (Chivers Large Print)
U.K. Softcover: 978 1 408 49396 0 (Camden Large Print)

Printed in the United States of America
1 2 3 4 5 6 7 14 13 12 11 10

For Arlene Tresness, a grandma like me, a lover of books, a devoted reader of mine. Thank you for your unfailing support and enthusiasm. (Your grandchildren think the world of you!)

PROLOGUE

"Is our ad there?" Fifteen-year-old Lindsey Remington whispered to her best friend. She glanced nervously at her bedroom door. Lindsey's biggest fear was that her mother would find her and Brenda scanning the Dateline section of the Wednesday paper and discover what they'd done.

Okay, so it was a bit . . . dishonest to write an ad on Meg Remington's behalf, but it was clear to Lindsey that her mom needed help. She was convinced that Meg *wanted* to remarry, whether she knew it or not.

It wasn't as if Lindsey could pull a potential husband out of nowhere. So she wrote the ad, with her best friend advising her.

"Here," Brenda said excitedly, pointing to the middle of the page. "It's here. Oh, my goodness! It's really here, just the way we wrote it."

Lindsey found the ad. She read aloud:

"Wanted: Perfect partner. I'm dating-shy,

divorced and seeking a man with marriage in mind. I look like a beauty queen, cook like a mom, kiss like a woman in love. Box 1234."

"It sounds even better in print," Brenda said.

"Do you think anyone will actually respond?" Lindsey asked.

"I bet we get lots of letters."

"I still think we should've said her kisses taste better than chocolate."

"It didn't fit. Remember?" They'd worked long and hard on the wording. Lindsey had wanted to describe her mother as "stunning," and Brenda was afraid it might not meet the truth-in-advertising rules.

All right, so her mother wasn't fashion model material, but she was very pretty. Or she could be, with a little assistance from the magazines Lindsey had been reading lately. Luckily Meg had a daughter who knew the ropes.

"Don't worry, Linds," Brenda said with a romantic sigh. "This is the best thing you could ever have done for your mother."

Lindsey hoped her mom appreciated her efforts. "Just remember, this guy has to be *perfect*. We'll need to be careful who we pick."

"No problem. If we don't like the sound

of one guy, we'll choose someone else," Brenda said, as if they were guaranteed to have tons of applicants. "That's the beauty of our plan. We'll screen all the applicants before your mother has a chance to date them. How many teenagers get to choose their own stepfathers? Not many, I bet."

Lindsey returned her attention to the ad, gnawing on the corner of her lip. She was experiencing a twinge of pride along with a mild case of guilt.

Her mother wasn't going to like this. When Meg learned what she and Brenda had done, she'd probably get all bent out of shape.

As for the ad, Lindsey figured if she were a man inclined to read the Dateline section, the ad would intrigue her.

"Some men will write just because your mom's pretty, but it's the part about her being a good cook that'll really work," Brenda assured her. "My grandma says Grandpa married her because her German potato salad was so good. Can you believe it?"

Brenda brought up a good point. "How will we know if a man is marrying her for her looks or her meat loaf or 'cause he loves her?"

"We won't," Brenda said, "but by then

we'll be out of the picture. Your mother will be on her own."

Lindsey wished she knew more about men. Unfortunately her experience was limited. She'd only gone on two real dates, both times to school dances. And her mother had been a chaperone.

"The day will come when Mom will appreciate what we've done for her," Lindsey said. "She's the one who's always saying how important it is to go after your dreams. Well, this is my dream for her. She wants a man. She just doesn't know it yet."

"All she needs is a little help from us."

"And she's got it," Lindsey said, smiling broadly.

ONE

Those girls were up to something. Meg Remington peeked in her fifteen-year-old daughter's bedroom to see Lindsey and her best friend, Brenda, crouched on the floor beside the bed. They were speaking in heated whispers.

Meg cleared her throat and instantly both girls were silent.

"Hi, Mom," Lindsey said, her bright blue eyes flashing.

Meg knew the look, which generally spelled trouble. "What are you two doing?"

"Nothing."

"Nothing," Brenda echoed with angelic innocence.

Meg crossed her arms and leaned her shoulder against the doorjamb. She had all the time in the world, and she wanted them to know it. "Tell me why I don't believe that. You two have the *look*."

"What look?" Lindsey repeated, turning

to Brenda.

"The one every mother recognizes. You're up to something, and I want to know what." She crossed her ankles, indicating that she'd make herself comfortable until they were ready to let her in on their little secret. She could outwait them if need be.

"All right, if you *must* know," Lindsey said with a shrug of defeat. She leapt to her feet and Brenda followed suit. "But we haven't finished planning everything yet."

"I must know." Meg was struck by how beautiful her daughter had become over the past few years. She'd gone from the gangly, awkward, big-teeth stage to real beauty almost overnight. Meg's ex-husband, Dave, had commented on the changes in Lindsey when she'd flown from Seattle to Los Angeles to visit over spring break. Their little girl was growing up.

"We've been doing some heavy-duty planning," Brenda explained.

"And exactly what are the two of you working on? I haven't seen you all evening." Generally, when Brenda stayed over, which was at least one night of every weekend, the two of them were up until all hours playing music, watching television or DVDs. The house had been suspiciously quiet all evening. Come to think of it, they'd been spending a lot of time in Lindsey's bedroom of late. Far too much time.

The girls glanced at each other before answering.

"You tell her," Brenda urged, "she's your mother."

"I know." Lindsey brushed back the long strands of hair. "But it might be a little easier coming from you."

"Lindsey?" Meg was more curious than ever now.

"You'd better sit down, Mom." Lindsey took Meg by the hand and guided her to the bed.

Meg sat on the edge. Both girls stood in front of her and each seemed to be waiting for the other to speak first.

"You're such an attractive woman," Lindsey began.

Meg frowned. This sounded like a setup to her, and the best way to handle that was to get straight to the point. "You need money? How much, and for what?"

With her usual flair for the dramatic, Lindsey rolled her eyes. "I don't need any money. I meant what I said — you're beautiful."

"It's true," Brenda piped up. "And you're only thirty-seven."

"I am?" Meg had to think about that.

"Yeah, I guess I am."

"You're still so young."

"I wouldn't go that far . . ."

"You've still got it, Mrs. Remington," Brenda cut in, her voice intense. "You're young and pretty and single, and you've got *it*." Her fist flew through the air and punctuated the comment.

"Got what?" Meg was beginning to feel a bit confused.

"You're not in bad shape, either," Lindsey commented, resting her chin on one hand.

Meg sucked in her stomach, feeling pleased with the girls' assessment.

"Of course you'd look even better if you lost ten pounds," her daughter said thoughtfully.

Ten pounds. Meg breathed again and her stomach pouched out. Those ten pounds had first made their appearance when Meg was pregnant with Lindsey nearly sixteen years earlier. She was downright proud of having maintained her post-pregnancy weight for all these years.

"Ten pounds isn't too much to lose," Brenda said confidently.

"It won't be hard at all — especially with the two of us helping you."

Meg stared into their eager, expectant faces. "Why is it so important for me to lose ten pounds? I happen to like the way I look."

"There's more."

Meg glanced from one girl to the other. "More? What is that supposed to mean?"

"You need to be physically fit. Think about it, Mom. When's the last time you ran an eight-minute mile?"

Meg didn't need to consider that at all — she already knew the answer. "Never." She'd jogged around the track during high school, only because it was required of her. The lowest grade she'd ever received was in phys ed.

"See?" Lindsey said to Brenda.

"We'll work with her," Brenda answered. "But we'll have to start soon."

Lindsey crossed her arms and carefully scrutinized Meg. "About your clothes, Mom."

"My clothes?" Meg cried, still astonished that her daughter wanted her to run an eight-minute mile. She owned a bookstore, for heaven's sake. In the eight years since she'd bought out Mr. Olsen, not once had she been required to run for anything.

"I want to know what's going on here," Meg said. "Now."

"I promise we'll answer all your questions in a minute," Brenda explained. "Please be patient, Mrs. Remington."

Lindsey sighed. "Mom, I don't mean to be rude or anything, but when it comes to your clothes, well . . . you need help."

"Help?" And to think Meg had been dressing herself for the past thirty-some years. Until now, no one had bothered to tell her what a poor job she'd done.

"I'm here to see you don't ever wear high-waisted jeans again," Lindsey said, as though pledging her life to a crusade. "They're called mom jeans," she whispered.

"So you two are official members of the fashion police?" Meg asked. Apparently they'd issued an APB on her!

Lindsey and Brenda giggled.

"That's what it sounds like."

"We're here to help you," Brenda said in loving tones.

"We're here to keep you from committing those fashion sins."

"What sins?" Meg should've known. "Do you mind telling me what this little heart-to-heart is all about?"

"*You,* Mom," Lindsey said, in a voice that suggested the answer should've been obvious.

"Why now? Why me?"

"Why not?" Lindsey responded.

Meg started to get up, but Lindsey directed her back onto the bed. "We aren't

16

finished yet. We're just getting to the good part."

"Honey, I appreciate what you're doing, but . . ."

"Sit down, Mom," Lindsey said in stern tones. "I haven't told you the most important thing yet."

Meg held up both hands. "Okay, okay."

"Like we already said, you're still young," Brenda began.

Lindsey smiled sweetly. "You could have more children if you wanted and —"

"Now wait a minute!" Meg cried.

"What we're really saying is that you're quite attractive."

"Or I could be," Meg amended, "with a little assistance from the two of you."

"Not all that much," Brenda added sympathetically. "We just want to get you started on the right track."

"I see," Meg muttered.

"Together," Lindsey said, slipping her arm around Brenda's waist and beaming a proud smile, "we're going to find you a husband."

"A husband." Meg's feet went out from under her and she slipped off the bed and landed with a solid whack on the carpet.

Lindsey and Brenda each grabbed one arm and pulled her off the floor. "Are you all right?" Lindsey asked, sounding genuinely concerned.

"You should've been more subtle," Brenda said accusingly. "There was no need to blurt it out like that."

Meg rubbed her rear end and sat back down on the bed. "What makes either of you think I want a husband?" she demanded angrily. She'd already been through one bad marriage and she wasn't eager to repeat the experience.

"When's the last time you went out on a date?" Lindsey asked.

"I don't remember," Meg snapped. "What does it matter, anyway?"

"Mother, it's clear to me you aren't thinking about the future."

"The future? What are you talking about?"

"Do you realize that in three years I'll be in college?"

"Three years," Meg repeated. "No-o, I guess I hadn't given it much thought." Although at the moment sending her daughter away actually seemed appealing.

"You'll be all alone."

"Alone isn't such a bad thing," Meg told them.

"At forty it is," Lindsey said dramatically. "I'll worry myself sick about you," she continued.

"She will," Brenda confirmed, nodding twice.

Meg figured it was a good thing she was sitting down.

"Tell me, Mother," Lindsey said, "what would it hurt to start dating again?"

"Honey, has it ever occurred to you that I'm happy just the way I am?"

"No," Lindsey returned. "You aren't happy. You're letting life pass you by. It's time to take action. I don't know what went wrong between you and Dad, but whatever it was must've been traumatic. You haven't had a relationship since — have you?"

Meg didn't answer that question, but wanted to reassure Lindsey about the break-up of her marriage. "It was a friendly divorce." In fact, Meg got along better with Dave now than she had when they were married.

Brenda shook her head. "There's no such thing as a friendly divorce. My dad's an attorney and he should know."

"I don't want to talk about the divorce," Meg said in her sternest voice. "It happened a long time ago and bringing it up now isn't going to help anyone."

"It might help *you*," Lindsey said, her eyes intense, "but I can understand why you don't want to talk about it. Don't worry," she said, and a bright smile transformed her face, "because you're going to get all the help you need from Brenda and me."

"That's what I was afraid of." Meg stood up and moved toward the door.

"Your diet starts tomorrow," Lindsey called after her.

"And your exercise regime," Brenda added. "You haven't got a thing to worry about, Mrs. Remington. We're going to find you a man before you know it."

Meg closed her eyes. If thirty-seven was so young, why didn't she have the energy to stand up to these two? She wasn't going on any diet, nor did she have time for exercising.

As for having Lindsey as a wardrobe consultant . . . That was ridiculous, and Meg intended to tell her daughter and Brenda exactly that.

First thing in the morning.

Meg soon learned exactly how serious Lindsey and Brenda were about finding her a husband. She woke Saturday morning to the sound of a workout DVD playing loudly on the television in her bedroom.

She lay facedown, awakened from a pleasant dream about a sunny beach. Her arm hung over the side of the bed, her fingertips dangling an inch or so above the carpet.

"You ready, Mrs. Remington?" Brenda called from the doorway.

She tried to ignore the girl, but that didn't work.

"You ready?" Brenda called a second time. She seemed to be jogging in place. "Don't worry, we'll go nice and slow in the beginning."

"I'm not doing anything without speaking to my attorney first," Meg muttered. She stuck out her arm and searched blindly for the phone.

"Forget it, Mom. That isn't going to work." Lindsey walked into the bedroom and set a coffee mug on the nightstand.

"Bless you, my child," Meg said. "Ah, coffee." She'd struggled into a sitting position before she realized caffeine had nothing to do with whatever Lindsey had brought her. "What *is* this?" she barked.

"It's a protein supplement. The lady at the health food store recommends it for toning skin in women over thirty."

"Are you sure you're supposed to drink it?" Meg asked.

Lindsey and Brenda looked at each other blankly.

"I'd better check the instructions again," Lindsey said and carried it away.

"Don't worry, Mrs. Remington, we'll have you whipped into shape in no time."

"Coffee," she pleaded. She couldn't be expected to do anything, let alone exercise, without caffeine.

"You can have your coffee," Brenda promised her, "but first . . ."

Meg didn't bother to listen to the rest. She slithered back under the covers and pulled a pillow over her head. Although it did block out some of the noise, she had no trouble hearing the girls. They weren't accepting defeat lightly. They launched into a lively discussion about the pros and cons of allowing Meg to drink coffee. She had news for these two dictators. Let either one of them try to stand between her and her first cup of coffee.

The conversation moved to the topic of the divorce; Brenda apparently believed Meg had suffered psychological damage that had prevented her from pursuing another relationship.

It was all Meg could do not to shove the pillow aside and put in her two cents' worth. What she should've done was order them out of the bedroom, but she was actually curious to hear what they had to say.

Her divorce hadn't been as bad as all that. She and Dave had made the mistake of marrying far too young. Meg had been twenty-two when she'd had Lindsey, and Dave was fresh out of college. In the five years of their marriage there hadn't been any ugly fights or bitter disagreements. Maybe it would've helped if there had been.

By the time Lindsey was four, Dave had decided he didn't love Meg anymore and wanted a divorce. It shouldn't have come as a surprise, but it did — and it hurt. Meg suspected he'd found someone else.

She was right.

For a long time after the divorce was final, Meg tried to convince herself that her failed marriage didn't matter. She and her husband had parted on friendly terms. For Lindsey's sake, Meg had made sure they maintained an amicable relationship.

Dave had hurt her, though, and Meg had denied that pain for too long. Eventually she'd recovered. It was over now, and she was perfectly content with her life.

She'd started working at Book Ends, an independent bookstore, and then, with a loan from her parents she'd managed to buy it.

Between the bookstore and a fifteen-year-old daughter, Meg had little time for seeking out new relationships. The first few years after the divorce she'd had a number of opportunities to get involved with other men. She hadn't. At the time, Meg simply wasn't interested, and as the years went on, she'd stopped thinking about it.

"Mother, would you please get out of this bed," Lindsey said, standing over her. Then in enticing tones, she murmured, "I have coffee."

"You tricked me before."

"This one's real coffee. The other stuff, well, I apologize about that. I guess I misunderstood the lady at the health food store. You were right. According to the directions, you're supposed to use it in the bath, not drink it. Sorry about that."

Meg could see it wasn't going to do the least bit of good to hide her face under a pillow. "I can't buy my way out of this?" she asked.

"Nope."

"You'll feel much better after you exercise," Brenda promised her. "Really, you will."

An hour later, Meg didn't feel any such thing. She couldn't move without some part of her anatomy protesting.

"You did great, Mrs. Remington," Brenda praised.

Meg limped into her kitchen and slowly lowered herself into a chair. Who would've believed a workout DVD, followed by a short — this was the term the girls used — one-mile run, would reduce her to this. In the past hour she'd been poked, prodded, pushed and punished.

"I've got your meals all planned out for you," Lindsey informed her. She opened the refrigerator door and took out a sandwich bag. She held it up for Meg's inspection. "This is your lunch."

Meg would've asked her about the meager contents if she'd had the breath to do so. All she could see was one radish, a square of cheese — low-fat, she presumed — and a small bunch of seedless grapes.

"Don't have any more than the nonfat yogurt for breakfast, okay?"

Meg nodded, rather than dredge up the energy to argue.

"Are you going to tell her about dinner?" Brenda asked.

"Oh, yeah. Listen, Mom, you've been a real trooper about this and we thought we should reward you. Tonight for dinner you can have a baked potato."

She managed a weak smile. Visions of butter and sour cream waltzed through her head.

"With fresh grilled fish."

"You like fish don't you, Mrs. Remington?"

Meg nodded. At this point she would've agreed to anything just to get the girls out of her kitchen, so she could recover enough to cook herself a decent breakfast.

"Brenda and I are going shopping," Lindsey announced. "We're going to pick out a whole new wardrobe for you, Mom."

"It's the craziest thing," Meg told her best friend, Laura Harrison, that same afternoon. They were unpacking boxes of books in the back room. "All of a sudden, Lindsey said she wants me to remarry."

"Really?"

Laura found this far too humorous to suit Meg. "But she wants me to lose ten pounds and run an eight-minute mile first."

"Oh, I get it now," Laura muttered, taking paperbacks from the shipping carton and placing them on a cart.

"What?"

"Lindsey was in the store a couple of weeks ago looking for a book that explained carbs and fat grams."

"I'm allowed thirty fat grams a day," Meg informed her. "And one hundred grams of carbohydrates." Not that her fifteen-year-old daughter was going to dictate what she

26

did and didn't eat.

"I hope Lindsey doesn't find out about that submarine sandwich you had for lunch."

"I couldn't help it," Meg said. "I haven't been that hungry in years. I don't think anyone bothered to tell Lindsey and Brenda that one of the effects of a workout is a voracious appetite."

"What was that phone call about earlier?" Laura asked.

Meg frowned as she moved books onto the cart. "Lindsey wanted my credit card number for a slinky black dress with a scoop neckline." Lindsey had sounded rapturous over the dress, describing it in detail, especially the deep cuts up the sides that would reveal plenty of thigh. "She said she found it on sale — and it was a deal too good to pass up." She paused. "Needless to say, I told her no."

"What would Lindsey want with a slinky black dress?"

"She wanted it for me," Meg said, under her breath.

"You?"

"Apparently once I fit the proper image, they plan to dress me up and escort me around town."

Laura laughed.

"I'm beginning to think you might not be such a good friend after all," Meg told her employee. "I expected sympathy and advice, not laughter."

"I'm sorry, Meg. Really."

She sounded far more amused than she did sorry.

Meg cast her a disgruntled look. "You know what your problem is, don't you?"

"Yes," Laura was quick to tell her. "I'm married, with college-age children. I don't have to put up with any of this nonsense and you do. Wait, my dear, until Lindsey gets her driver's license. *Then* you'll know what real fear is."

"One disaster at a time, thank you." Meg sat on a stool and reached for her coffee cup. "I don't mind telling you I'm worried about all this."

"Why?" Laura straightened and picked up her own cup, refilling it from the freshly brewed pot. "It's a stage Lindsey's going through. Trust me, it'll pass."

"Lindsey keeps insisting I'll be lonely when she leaves for college, which she reminded me is in three years."

"Will you be?"

Meg had to think about that. "I don't know. I suppose in some ways I will be. The house will feel empty without her." The two weeks Lindsey spent with her father every year seemed interminable. Meg wandered around the house like a lost puppy.

"So, why *not* get involved in another relationship?" Laura asked.

"With whom?" was Meg's first question. "I don't know any single men."

"Sure you do," Laura countered. "There's Ed, who has the insurance office two doors down."

"Ed's single?" She rather liked Ed. He seemed like a decent guy, but she'd never thought of him in terms of dating.

"The fact that you didn't know Ed was single says a lot. You've got to keep your eyes and ears open."

"Who else?"

"Buck's divorced."

Buck was a regular customer, and although she couldn't quite understand why, Meg had never cared for him. "I wouldn't go out with Buck."

"I didn't say you had to go out with him, I just said he was single."

Meg couldn't see herself kissing either man. "Anyone else?"

"There are lots of men out there."

"Oh, really, and I'm blind?"

"Yes," Laura said. "If you want the truth, I don't think Lindsey's idea is so bad. True, she may be going about it the wrong way, but it wouldn't hurt you to test the waters. You might be surprised at what you find."

Meg sighed. She'd expected support from her best friend, and instead Laura had turned traitor.

By the time Meg had closed the bookstore and headed home, she was exhausted. So much for all those claims about exercise generating energy. In her experience, it did the reverse.

"Lindsey," she called out, "are you home?"

"I'm in my room," came the muffled reply from the bedroom at the top of the stairs.

Something she couldn't put her finger on prompted Meg to hurry upstairs to her daughter's bedroom despite her aching muscles. She knocked once and opened the door to see Lindsey and Brenda sitting on the bed, leafing through a stack of letters.

Lindsey hid the one she was reading behind her back. "Mom?" she said, her eyes wide. "Hi."

"Hello."

"Hello, Mrs. Remington," Brenda said, looking decidedly guilty.

It was then that Meg saw the black dress hanging from the closet door. It was the most provocative thing she'd seen in years.

"How'd you get the dress?" Meg demanded, angry that Lindsey had gone against her wishes and wondering how she'd managed to do it.

The two girls stared at each other, neither one eager to give her an answer. "Brenda phoned her mother and she put it on her credit card," Lindsey said at last.

"What?" Meg felt ready to explode.

"It was only a small lie," Brenda said quickly. "I told my mom it was perfect and on sale and too cheap to resist. What I didn't tell her was that the dress wasn't for me."

"It's going back right this minute, and then the three of us are paying Brenda's parents a visit."

"Mom!" Lindsey flew off the bed. "Wait, please." She had a panicked look in her eyes. "What we did was wrong, but when you wouldn't agree to buy the dress yourself, we didn't know what to do. You just don't have anything appropriate for Chez Michelle."

Chez Michelle was one of the most exclusive restaurants in Seattle, with a reputation for excellent French cuisine. Meg had never eaten there herself, but Laura and her husband had celebrated their silver wedding anniversary at Chez Michelle and raved about it for weeks afterward.

31

"You're not making any sense," Meg told her daughter.

Lindsey bit her lip and nodded.

"You have to tell her," Brenda insisted.

"Tell me what?"

"You're the one who wrote the last letter," Lindsey said. "The least you could've done was get the dates right."

"It's tonight."

"I know," Lindsey snapped.

"Would someone tell me what's going on here?" Meg asked, her patience at its end.

"You need that dress, Mom," Lindsey said in a voice so low Meg had to strain to hear her.

"And why would that be?"

"You have a dinner date."

"I do? And just who am I going out with?" She assumed this had something to do with Chez Michelle.

"Steve Conlan."

"Steve Conlan?" Meg repeated. She said it again, looking for something remotely familiar about the name and finding nothing,

"You don't know him," Lindsey told her. "But he's really nice. Brenda and I both like him." She glanced at her friend for confirmation and Brenda nodded eagerly.

"You've met him?" Meg didn't like the

32

sound of this.

"Not really. We exchanged a couple of letters and then we e-mailed back and forth
and he seems like a really great guy." The
last part was said with forced enthusiasm.

"You've been writing a strange man."

"He's not so strange, Mom, not really. He
sounds just like one of us."

"He wants to meet you," Brenda put in.

"Me?" Meg brought her hand to her
throat. "Why would he want to do that?"

The girls shared a look, reminiscent of the
one she'd caught the night before.

"Lindsey?" Meg asked. "Why would this
man want to meet me?"

Her daughter lowered her eyes, refusing
to meet Meg's. "Because when we wrote
Steve . . ."

"Yes?"

"Brenda and I told him we were you."

TWO

Steve Conlan glanced at his watch. The time hadn't changed since he'd looked before. He could tell it was going to be one of those nights. He had the distinct feeling it would drag by, one interminable minute after another.

He still hadn't figured how he'd gotten himself into this mess. He was minding his own business and the next thing he knew . . . He didn't want to think about it, because whenever he did his blood pressure rose.

Nancy was going to pay for this.

He was early, not because he was so eager for tonight. No, he was only eager to get it over with.

He tried not to check the time and failed. A minute had passed. Or was it a lifetime?

His necktie felt as if it would strangle him. A tie. He couldn't believe he'd let Nancy talk him into wearing a stupid tie.

Because he needed something to occupy

34

his time, he took the snapshot out of his shirt pocket.

Meg Remington.

She had a nice face, he decided. Nothing spectacular. She certainly wasn't drop-dead gorgeous, but she wasn't plain, either. Her eyes were her best feature. Clear. Bright. Expressive. She had a cute mouth, too. Very kissable. Sensuous.

What was he supposed to say to the woman? The hell if he knew. He'd read her letters and e-mails a dozen times. She sounded — he hated to say it — immature, as if she felt the need to impress him. She seemed to think that because she ran an eight-minute mile it qualified her for the Olympics. Frankly, he wondered what their dinner would be like, with her being so food conscious and all. She'd actually bragged about how few fat grams and carbs she consumed. Clearly she wasn't familiar with the menu at Chez Michelle. He couldn't see a single low-fat or low-carb entrée.

That was another thing. The woman had expensive tastes. Dinner at Chez Michelle would set him back three hundred bucks — if he was lucky. So far he'd been anything but . . .

Involuntarily his gaze fell to his watch again, and he groaned inwardly. His sister owed him for this.

Big time.

"I refuse to meet a strange man for dinner," Meg insisted coldly. There were some things even a mother wouldn't do.

"But you have to," Brenda pleaded. "I'm sorry, Mrs. Remington, I feel really bad springing this on you, but Steve didn't do anything wrong. You've just *got* to show up. You have to . . . otherwise he might lose faith in all women."

"So?"

"But he's your date," Lindsey said. "It would've worked out great if . . ." she paused and scowled at her best friend ". . . if one of us hadn't gotten the days mixed up."

"Exactly when did you plan on telling me you've been communicating with a strange man, using *my* name?"

"Soon," Lindsey said with conviction. "We had to . . . He started asking about meeting you almost right away. We did everything we could to hold him off. Oh, by the way, if he asks about your appendix, you've made a full recovery."

Meg groaned. The time frame of their deception wasn't what interested her. She was stalling, looking for a way out of this.

She could leave a message for Steve at the restaurant, explaining that she couldn't make it, but that seemed like such a cowardly thing to do.

Unfortunately no escape plan presented itself. Brenda was right; it wasn't Steve's fault that he'd been duped by a pair of teenagers. It wasn't her fault, either, but then Lindsey was her daughter.

"He's very nice-looking," Brenda said. She reached behind her and pulled out a picture from one of the envelopes scattered across Lindsey's bed. "Here, see what I mean?" Meg swore she heard the girl sigh. "He's got blue eyes and check out his smile."

Meg took the photo from Brenda and studied it. Her daughter's friend was right. Steve Conlan was pleasant-looking. His hair was a little long, but that didn't bother her. He wore a cowboy hat and boots and had his thumbs tucked into his hip pockets as he stared into the camera.

"He's tall, dark and *lonesome*," Lindsey said wistfully.

"Has he ever been married?" Meg asked, curiosity getting the better of her.

"Nope." This time it was Brenda who supplied the information. "He's got his own business, same as you, Mrs. Remington. He owns a body shop and he's been sinking every penny into it."

"What made him place the ad?" she asked the girls. A sudden thought came to her. "He *is* the one who advertised, isn't he?"

Both girls looked away and Meg's heart froze. "You mean to say you two advertised for a husband for me?" She spoke slowly, each word distinct.

"We got lots of letters, too," Brenda said proudly. "We went through them all and chose Steve Conlan."

"Don't you want to know why?" Lindsey prodded.

Meg gestured weakly, still too shocked to react.

"Steve says he decided to answer your ad because one day he woke up and realized life was passing him by. All his friends were married, and he felt like something important was missing in his life. Then he knew it wasn't *something* but someone."

"What about female friends?" Meg asked, thinking he didn't look like a man who'd have to find companionship in the classifieds.

"He said in his letter that . . ." Lindsey paused and rustled through a sheaf of papers, searching for the right envelope. "Here it is," she muttered. "He doesn't have much opportunity to meet single women unless they've been in an accident, and generally they're not in the mood for romance when they're dealing with a body shop and an insurance company." Lindsey grinned. "He's kind of witty. I like that about him."

"He said a lot of women his age have already been married and divorced and had a passel of kids."

This didn't sound too promising to Meg. "You did happen to mention that I'm divorced, too, didn't you?"

"Of course," Lindsey insisted. "We'd never lie."

Meg bit her tongue to keep from saying the obvious.

"Just think," Brenda said, "out of all the women who advertised, Steve chose you and we chose him. It's destiny."

The girls thought she'd feel complimented, but Meg was suspicious. "Surely there was someone younger and prettier, without children, who interested him."

The two girls exchanged a smile. "He liked the fact that you count carbs and fat grams," Brenda said proudly.

So much for their unwillingness to stretch the truth. "You actually told him that?" She closed her eyes and groaned. "What else did you say?"

"Just that you're really wonderful."

"Heroic," Brenda added. "And you are."

Oh, great. They'd made her sound like a thin Joan of Arc.

"You will meet him, won't you?" Lindsey's dark eyes pleaded with Meg.

"What I should do is march the two of you down to that fancy restaurant and have you personally apologize to him. You both deserve to be grounded until you're forty."

The girls blinked in unison. "But, Mom . . ."

"Mrs. Remington . . ."

Meg raised her hand and stopped them. "I won't take you to Chez Michelle, and as for the grounding part . . . we'll discuss it later."

Two pairs of shoulders sagged with relief.

"But I won't have dinner with Steve Conlan," she said emphatically. "I'll go to the restaurant, introduce myself and explain what happened. I'm sure he'll agree that the best thing to do is skip dinner altogether."

"You'll wear the dress, won't you?" Lindsey asked, eyeing the slinky black concoction hanging outside her closet door.

"Absolutely not," Meg said. She refused to even consider it.

"But you don't have anything special

enough for Chez Michelle. Just try it on, Mom."

"No. Well . . ."

"Come on, Mom. Brenda and I want to see how it looks."

An hour later Meg pulled up at Chez Michelle in the very dress she'd sworn she'd never wear. It fit as if it'd been designed just for her, enhancing her figure and camouflaging those stubborn ten pounds. At least that was what Lindsey and Brenda told her.

"Hello." The hostess greeted her with a wide smile. "Table for one?"

"I'm . . . meeting someone," Meg said, glancing around the waiting area looking for a man who resembled "tall, dark and lonesome" in the photo. No one did. Nor was there a single male wearing a cowboy hat.

The only man who looked vaguely like the one in the photograph stood in the corner of the room, leaning indolently against the wall as if he had all the time in the world.

He straightened and stared at her.

Meg stared back.

He reached inside his suit pocket and took out a picture.

Meg opened the clasp of her purse and removed the photo the girls had given her.

She looked down at it and then up again.

He appeared to be doing the same thing.

"Meg Remington?" he asked uncertainly.

She nodded. "Steve Conlan?"

He nodded, too.

He wore a suit and tie. A suit and tie. The guy had really gone all out for her. Meg swallowed uncomfortably. He'd invited her to this ultrafancy restaurant expecting to meet the woman who'd exchanged those letters and messages with him. Meg felt her heart settle somewhere in the vicinity of her knees. She couldn't very well introduce herself and immediately say it had all been a mistake and cancel dinner. Not when he'd gone to so much trouble.

"I believe our table is ready," Steve said, holding out his arm to her. His hand touched her elbow and he addressed the hostess. "We can be seated now."

The woman gave him an odd look, then picked up two huge menus. "This way."

Meg might've been wrong, but she thought she heard some reluctance in his voice. Perhaps she was a disappointment to Steve Conlan. After the fitness drill Lindsey and Brenda had put her through, Meg was feeling her advancing age.

Pride stiffened Meg's shoulders. So she hadn't signed any modeling contracts lately.

What did he expect from a thirty-seven-year-old woman? If he wanted to date a woman in her twenties, he shouldn't have answered her ad. Lindsey's ad, she corrected. It was all Meg could do not to stop Steve Conlan right then and there and tell him this was as good as it got.

Especially in this dress. It was simply gorgeous. Meg knew now the girls had made the perfect choice. She was glad she'd given in to them on this one. Besides, Lindsey was right; she didn't own anything fancy enough for Chez Michelle. Before she could stop herself she'd agreed to wear it. Soon both girls were offering her fashion advice.

They were escorted to a linen-covered table next to the window, which overlooked Elliot Bay and Puget Sound. The moon's reflection on the water sent gilded light across the surface, and the restaurant's interior was dimly lit.

Meg squinted, barely able to read her menu. She wondered if Steve was having the same problem. Originally she hadn't intended to have dinner with him. Wouldn't even now, if he hadn't gone to so much trouble on her behalf. It seemed crass to drop in, announce it had all been a misguided attempt by her daughter to play matchmaker, ask his forgiveness and speed-

43

ily disappear.

"I believe I'll have the chicken cordon bleu," she said, deciding on the least expensive item on the menu. "And please, I insist on paying for my own meal." It would be unforgivable to gouge him for that as well.

"Dinner's on me," Steve insisted, setting his menu aside. He smiled for the first time and it transformed his face. He studied her, as if he wasn't sure what to make of her.

"But . . ." Meg lowered her gaze and closed her mouth. She didn't know where to start and yet she didn't know how much longer she could maintain the pretense. "This is all very elegant. . . ."

"Yes," he agreed, spinning the stem of his water glass between his thumb and index finger.

"You look different than your picture." Meg had no idea why she'd told him that. What she *should* be doing was explaining about Lindsey and Brenda.

"How's that?"

"Your eyes are much bluer and you've cut your hair."

He gave a slight grin. "And your picture didn't do you justice."

Meg hadn't thought to ask Lindsey which one she'd mailed Steve. "Can I see?"

"Sure." He pulled it out of his pocket and

44

handed it over.

Meg took one look and rolled her eyes. She couldn't believe Lindsey had sent this particular photograph to anyone. It'd been taken just before Christmas a year earlier. She was standing in front of the Christmas tree wearing a white dress that drained all the color from her face. The flash from the camera made her eyes appear red. She looked like she was recovering from a serious ailment.

"This is one of the worst pictures ever taken of me," she said impatiently. "The one of me at the bookstore is *much* better."

Steve's brow creased with a frown. "I see. You should've sent that one."

Meg realized what she'd said too late. "You're right, I should have. . . . How silly of me."

The waitress came and they placed their orders, both declining a drink, Meg to keep down the cost and Steve, no doubt, to hurry the meal along.

Once the server had left the table, Meg carefully smoothed the napkin across her lap. "Listen, Steve . . ."

"Meg . . ."

They both stopped.

"You go first," he said, gesturing toward her.

"All right." She cocked her head to one side and then the other, going over the words in her mind. "This isn't easy. . . ."

Steve frowned. "It's been a pleasure to meet me, but the chemistry just isn't there and you'd like to let me down gently and be done with it."

"No!" she hurried to assure him.

"Oh."

The disappointment in his tone came as a mild shock. Then she understood. "You . . . expected a different kind of woman and —"

"Not in the least. If the truth be known, I'm pleasantly surprised."

She swallowed. "I wish you hadn't said that."

"Why not?"

"Because . . ." She dragged in a deep breath. "Because I'm not the person you think I am. I mean . . ." This was proving even more difficult than it should have. "I didn't write those letters."

Steve's eyes narrowed. "Then who did?"

"My daughter and her friend."

"I . . . see."

Meg's fingers crushed the linen napkin in her lap. "You have every reason to be upset. It was an underhanded thing to do to us both."

"You didn't know anything about this?"

46

"I swear I didn't. I would've put a stop to it immediately if I had."

Steve reached for his water and drank thirstily. "I would have, too."

"I want you to know I intend to discipline Lindsey for this. I can only apologize . . ." She stopped midsentence when she saw his shoulders moving with suppressed laughter. "Steve?"

"I didn't write those letters, either. The ones from me."

"What?" Disbelief settled over Meg. "You mean to say you didn't respond to the ad in Dateline?"

"Nope. My romantic little sister did. Nancy's on this kick about seeing me married. I don't understand it, but —"

"Just a minute," Meg said, raising her hand. "Let me see if I've got this straight. You didn't place the ad in Dateline."

"You've got it."

"Then why are you here?"

He shrugged. "Probably for the same reason you are. I figured you were some lonely heart seeking companionship and frankly I felt bad that Nancy had led you on like this. It isn't your fault my crazy sister thinks it's time I got married."

He paused when their meals were delivered.

47

Meg dug into her chicken with gusto. Irritation usually made her hungry. She stabbed a carrot slice with her fork.

"So you felt sorry for me?" she said, chewing the carrot vigorously.

He looked up, apparently sensing her irritation. "No sorrier than you felt for me."

He had her there.

"It's the reason you showed up, isn't it?" he pressed.

She agreed with a nod. "When did you find out about this dinner date?"

"This morning. You?"

She glanced at her watch. "About two hours ago."

Steve chuckled. "They didn't give you much opportunity to object, did they?"

"Actually they got the days mixed up and went into a panic. I don't suppose you happened to read any of the letters or e-mails they wrote?"

"As a matter of fact I did. Interesting stuff."

"I'll bet." She stabbed one of the potato pieces with her fork. "You should know that not everything they said was the truth." She put the potato in her mouth and chewed.

"So you don't actually run an eight-minute mile."

"No . . ."

"Nine minutes?"

"I don't exactly run, and before you ask me about carbs and fat grams, you can forget everything Lindsey told you about those, too. And for the record, my appendix is in great shape."

Steve chuckled. "What did Nancy tell you about me?"

"Since I've only read tidbits of your letters and e-mails, I can't really say."

"Oh?" His voice fell noticeably.

"As I recall, your sister did suggest that your life's quite empty and you're looking for something to fill your lonely nights —" she paused for effect "— until you realized it wasn't *something* you were searching for but *someone*."

His jaw tightened. "She said that?"

"Yup." Meg took some pleasure in telling him that.

"Well, that's a crock of bull. I certainly hope you didn't believe it."

Meg smiled. "Not really. Lindsey didn't mean any harm, you know."

"Nancy, either, although I'd like to throttle her. The kid's nineteen and she's got romance and marriage on her mind. Unfortunately, it's me she's trying to marry off."

"Lindsey thinks I'm lost and lonely, but I'm perfectly content with my life."

"Me, too."

"Why ruin everything now?"

"Exactly," Steve agreed with conviction. "A woman would want to change everything about me."

"A man would string me along until he found someone prettier and sexier. Besides," Meg added, "I have no intention of becoming a pawn in some ploy of my daughter's."

"Nancy can take a flying leap into Green Lake before I'll let her arrange my love life," Steve told her adamantly. "I certainly intend to marry, but on *my* time — not when my kid sister ropes me into a lonely-hearts-club relationship."

"I feel the same way."

"Great." Steve grinned at her, and Meg had to admit he had a wonderful smile. It lit up his eyes and softened his features. "Shall we drink to our agreement?"

"Definitely."

Steve attracted the waitress's attention and ordered a bottle of wine.

Meg was astonished by the ease with which they could talk, once all the pretense between them had been resolved. She told him about her bookstore and liked hearing about his body shop. They lingered over coffee and dessert, and not until it became apparent that the restaurant was about to close did they get up to leave.

"I enjoyed myself," Meg said as they strolled to the door.

"Don't sound so surprised."

"Frankly, I am."

He laughed. "I guess I am, too."

The valet brought her Ford Escort to the front of the restaurant and held open her door.

"Thank you for a lovely dinner," she said, suddenly feeling shy and awkward.

"The pleasure was all mine."

Neither of them made an effort to move. The valet checked his watch and Meg glanced at him guiltily. Steve ignored him and eventually so did Meg.

"I guess this is goodbye," she said, wishing now that she hadn't made such a big issue about not being her daughter's pawn.

"Looks that way."

She lowered her eyes, fighting the enticement she read in his. "Thanks again."

Steve traced his finger along her jaw. His work-calloused fingertip felt warm against her skin. If they hadn't been standing under the lights of a fancy French restaurant with a valet looking on, Meg wondered if he would've kissed her. She wanted to think he might have.

On the drive home, she dismissed the idea

as fanciful. It had been a long time since she'd been wined and dined, that was all. And an even longer time since she'd been kissed . . .

Sensation after sensation traveled across her face where he'd touched her. Smile after smile flirted with her mouth at the memory of his lips so close to hers. She wouldn't forget the date or the man anytime soon. That was for sure.

"Well, how'd it go?" Nancy demanded. His teenage sister met Steve at the door. Her eyes were wide with curiosity as she followed him inside.

Steve looked at his watch and frowned. "What are you still doing up?"

Nancy's face fell. "You asked me to wait for you, so we could talk."

Steve slid his fingers through his hair. "I did, didn't I?"

"You're much later than you thought you'd be."

He didn't respond, unwilling to let his sister know how much he'd enjoyed himself. "I'm furious with you for what you did," he said, forcing his voice to sound gruff with irritation.

"I don't blame you," she agreed readily enough.

"Haven't you got an exam to study for or something?" he asked, although he knew very well she didn't. Nancy attended the nearby University of Washington. She was staying with Steve for the summer, since their parents were now living in Montana.

"You liked her, didn't you?"

Nancy sounded much too smug to suit Steve.

"And no, I don't have any exams to study for, and you know it. They ended two weeks ago." Since then, she'd taken a summer job at the university library.

"So you've decided to stay in Seattle and make my life miserable."

"No, I've decided to stay in Seattle and see you married. Come on, Steve, you're thirty-eight! That's getting up there." She flopped down on the sofa and sat with her legs underneath her, as if she planned to plant herself right there until he announced his engagement.

The problem, Steve decided, was that Nancy was the product of parents who'd never expected a second child and had spoiled her senseless. He was partially to blame, as well, but he'd never thought she'd pull something like this.

"You work too hard," she said. "Loosen up and enjoy life a little."

"You're going to write Meg Remington a formal letter of apology." He refused to back down on this.

"Okay, I'll write her." All at once she was on her feet. "When are you seeing her again?"

"I'm not."

Nancy fell back onto the sofa. "Why not?"

Darned if Steve could give her an answer. He and Meg had made that decision early on in their conversation, and for the life of him he couldn't remember why.

"Because," he growled. "Now leave me alone."

Nancy threw back her head and laughed. "You like her. You really, really like her."

Meg sat in the back storeroom and rubbed her aching feet. The new shoes pinched her toes, but this was what she got for buying them half a size too small. They were on sale and she loved them, although the store had been out of size eights. Even knowing her feet would pay the penalty later, Meg had chosen to wear them today.

Laura stuck her head through the door and smiled when she saw her. "A beautiful bouquet of flowers just arrived for you," she said.

"For me?"

"That's what the envelope said."

"Who from?"

"I didn't read the card, if that's what you're asking, but Lindsey's here and she grabbed it and let out a holler. My guess is the flowers are from Steve."

"Steve." Pain or no pain, Meg was on her feet. She hobbled to the front of the store and found her fifteen-year-old daughter grinning triumphantly.

"Steve Conlan sent flowers," she crowed.

"So I see." Meg's fingers shook as she removed the card from the small envelope.

"He said, and I quote, 'You're one special woman, Meg Remington. Love, Steve.' "

The bouquet was huge, with at least ten different varieties of flowers all arranged in a white wicker basket. It must have cost him easily a hundred dollars.

"We agreed," she whispered.

"Agreed to what?" Lindsey prodded.

"That we weren't going to see each other again."

"Obviously he changed his mind," Lindsey said, as excited as if she'd just discovered a twenty-dollar bill in the bottom of her purse.

Unwilling to trust her daughter's assessment of the situation, Meg stared at her best friend.

"Don't look at me," Laura said.

"I'm sure you're wrong," Meg said to Lindsey, her heart still beating a little too fast.

"Why else would he send flowers?" Lindsey asked calmly.

"He wanted to say he was glad we met, that's all. I don't think we should make something out of this," she said. "It's just . . . a courtesy."

"Call him," Lindsey pleaded.

"I most certainly will not!"

"But, Mom, don't you see? Steve's saying he likes you, but he doesn't want to pressure you into anything unless you like him, too."

"He is?" Whatever confidence she'd felt a moment earlier vanished like ice cream at a Fourth of July picnic.

"The next move is yours."

"Laura?"

"I wouldn't know," her fickle friend said. "I've been married to the same man for twenty-six years. All this intrigue is beyond me."

"I agree with your daughter," a shy voice said from the other side of the counter. "You should call him."

It was Meg's customer, Judith Wilson. Meg wasn't sure she should listen to the older woman who faithfully purchased romance novels twice a month. Judith was a real romantic and would undoubtedly read more into the gesture than Steve had intended.

"See?" Lindsey said excitedly. "The ball's in your court. Steve made his move and now he's waiting for yours."

Meg didn't know what to do.

"It's been three days," Lindsey reminded her. "He's had time to think over the situation, and so have you."

"Call him," Laura suggested. "If for nothing more than to thank him for the flowers."

"Yes, call him," Judith echoed, clutching her bag of books.

"It's the least you can do." Once more it was her daughter offering advice.

"All right," Meg said reluctantly. The flowers were gorgeous, and thanking him would be the proper thing to do.

"I'll get his work number for you," Lindsey volunteered, pulling the Yellow Pages from behind the cash register.

The kid had Steve's shop number faster than directory assistance could have located it.

"I'll use the phone in the back room," Meg said. She didn't need several pairs of ears listening in on her conversation.

She felt everyone's eyes on her as she hurried into the storeroom. Her hand actually shook as she punched out the telephone number.

"Emerald City," a gruff male voice answered.

"Hello, this is Meg Remington calling for Steve Conlan."

"Hold on a minute."

"Of course."

A moment later, Steve was on the line. "Meg?"

"Hello, Steve. I know you're busy, so I won't take up much of your time. I'm calling to thank you for the flowers."

A long pause followed her words. "Flowers? What flowers?"

THREE

"You mean you don't know anything about these flowers?" Meg cried, her voice raised. Steve could see that he hadn't done a very good job of breaking the news, but he was as shocked as she was.

"If you didn't send them, who did?" Meg demanded.

It wasn't difficult to figure that one out. "I can make a wild guess," he said with heavy sarcasm. He jerked his fingers through his hair, then glanced at the wall clock. It was close to quitting time. "Can you meet me?"

"Why?"

Her blatant lack of enthusiasm irritated him. He'd been thinking about her for three days. Nancy was right — he liked Meg Remington. She was a bit eccentric and a little on the hysterical side, but he was willing to overlook that. During their time together, he'd been struck by her intelligence and her warmth. He'd wished more than once that they'd decided to ignore the way they'd been thrown together and continue to see each other. Apparently Meg suffered no such regrets and was pleased to be rid of him.

"Why do you want to meet?" she repeated, lowering her voice.

"We need to talk."

"Where?"

"How about a drink? Can you get away from the store in the next hour or so?"

She hesitated. "I'll try."

Steve mentioned a popular sports bar in Kent, and she agreed to meet him there at five-thirty. His spirits lifted considerably at the prospect of seeing her again. He must've been smiling as he hung up because his foreman, Gary Wilcox, cast him a puzzled look.

"I didn't know you had yourself a new girlfriend," Gary said. "When did this happen?"

"It hasn't." The last thing Steve needed was Gary feeding false information to his sister. Nancy and her outrageous ideas about marrying him off was enough of a problem, without Gary encouraging it.

"It hasn't happened *yet,* you mean," Gary said, making a notation in the appointment schedule.

Steve glanced over his shoulder, to be sure Gary wasn't making notes about the conversation he'd had with Meg. He was getting paranoid already. A woman did that to a man, made him jumpy and insecure; he knew that much from past experience.

An hour later Steve sat in the bar, facing a big-screen television with a frosty mug of beer in his hand. The table he'd chosen was in the far corner of the room, where he could easily watch the front door.

Meg walked in ten minutes after him. At least Steve thought it was Meg. The woman carried a tennis racket and wore one of those cute little pleated-skirt outfits. He hadn't realized Meg played tennis. He knew she didn't run and disliked exercise, but . . .

Steve squinted and stared, unsure. After all, he'd only seen her the one time, and in the slinky black dress she'd looked a whole lot different.

Meg solved his problem when she apparently recognized him. She walked across the room, and he noticed that she was limping. She slid into the chair beside him, then set the tennis racket on the table.

"Lindsey knows," she announced.

Steve's head went back to study her. "I beg your pardon?"

"My daughter figured it out."

"Figured what out?"

"That I was meeting you," she said in exasperated tones. "First, I called you from the back room at the store, so our conversation could be private."

"So?"

She glared at him. "Then I made up this ridiculous story about a tennis game I'd forgotten. I haven't played tennis in years and Lindsey knows that. She immediately had all these questions. She saw straight through me." She pulled the sweatband from her hair and stuffed it in her purse. "She's probably home right now laughing her head off. I can't do this. . . . I could never lie convincingly."

"Why didn't you just tell your daughter the truth?" He was puzzled by the need to lie at all.

Meg's look of consternation said that would've been impossible. "Well . . . because Lindsey would think the two of us meeting meant something."

"Why? You told her I didn't write those letters and e-mails, didn't you?"

"No."

"Why not?"

Meg played with the worn strings of the tennis racket as her eyes avoided his. "I should have. . . . I mean, this is crazy."

"You can say that again." He tried to sound nonchalant and wondered if he'd managed it. He didn't think so. He was actually rather amused by the whole setup. Her daughter and his sister. The girls were close in age and obviously spoke the same language.

"Lindsey's still got romantic ideas when it comes to men and marriage, but . . ." Meg paused and chanced a look at him. "She really stepped over the line with this stunt."

"What did you say about our date?"

Meg's hands returned to the tennis racket. "Not much."

Steve hadn't been willing to discuss the details of their evening together with Nancy, either. Nothing had surprised him more than discovering how attractive he'd found Meg Remington. It wasn't solely a sexual attraction, although she certainly appealed to him.

Whenever he'd thought about her in the past three days, he'd remember how they'd talked nonstop over wine and dessert. He remembered how absorbed she'd been in what he was saying; at one point she'd leaned forward and then realized her dress revealed a fair bit of cleavage. Red-faced, she'd pulled back and attempted to adjust her bodice.

Steve liked the way her eyes brightened when she spoke about her bookstore and her daughter, and the way she had of holding her breath when she was excited about something, as if she'd forgotten to breathe.

"Your sister — the one who wrote the letters — is the same one who sent the flowers?" Meg asked, breaking into his thoughts.

Steve nodded. "I'd bet on it."

Meg fiddled with the clasp of her purse and brought out a small card, which she handed him.

Steve raised his arm to attract the cocktail waitress's attention and indicate he wanted another beer for Meg.

"I shouldn't," she said, reaching for a pretzel. "If I come home with beer on my breath, Lindsey will know for sure I wasn't playing tennis."

"According to you, she's already figured it out."

She slid the bowl of pretzels closer and grabbed another handful. "That's true."

Steve opened the card that had come with the flowers and rolled his eyes. "This is from Nancy, all right," he muttered. "I'd never write anything this hokey."

The waitress came with another mug of beer and Steve paid for it. "Do you want more pretzels?" he asked Meg.

"Please." Then in a lower voice, she added, "This type of situation always makes me hungry."

She licked the salt from her fingertips. "Has my daughter, Lindsey, been in contact with you?"

"No, but then I wouldn't know, would I?"

Meg was holding the pretzel in front of her mouth. "Why wouldn't you?"

"Because Lindsey would be writing to Nancy."

Meg's head dropped in a gesture of defeat. "You're right. Much more of this craziness and heaven only knows what they could do to our lives."

"We need to take control," Steve said.

"I totally agree with you," was her response. She took a sip of her beer and set the mug down. "I shouldn't be drinking this on an empty stomach — it'll go straight to my head."

"The bar's got great sandwiches."

"Pretzels are fine." Apparently she'd realized that she was holding the bowl, and she shoved it back to the center of the table. "Sorry," she muttered.

"No problem."

He saw her wince and recalled that she'd been limping earlier. "Is there something wrong with your foot?"

"The shoes I wore to work were too tight," she said, speaking so quietly he had to strain to hear.

"Here," he said, reaching under the table for her feet and setting them on his lap.

"What are you doing?" she asked in a shocked voice.

"I thought I'd rub them for you."

"You'd do that?"

"Yes." It didn't seem so odd to him. The fact was, he hated to see her in pain. "Besides, we need to talk over how we're going to handle this situation. I have a feeling that we'll have to be in top mental form to deal with these kids."

"You're right." She closed her eyes and purred like a well-fed kitten when he removed her tennis shoes and kneaded her aching feet.

"Feel better?" he asked after a couple of minutes.

She nodded, her eyes still closed. "I think you should stop," she said, sounding completely unconvincing.

"Why?" He asked the question, but he stopped and bent down to pick up her shoes, which he'd placed on the floor.

"Thank you," Meg said. She looked around a little self-consciously as she slipped her shoes back on and tied the laces.

Feeling somewhat embarrassed by his uncharacteristic response to her, Steve cleared his throat and picked up his beer. "Do you have any ideas?" he asked.

She stared at him as if she didn't know what he was talking about, then straightened abruptly. "Oh, you mean for dealing with the kids. No, not really. What about you? Any suggestions?"

"Well, we're agreed that we've got to stop letting them run our lives."

"Exactly. We can't allow them to force us into a relationship."

He nodded. But if that was the case, he wondered, why did he experience the almost overwhelming desire to kiss her? All of a sudden, it bothered him that they were discussing strategies that would ensure the end of any contact between them.

He imagined leaning toward her, touching his lips to hers. . . .

There's something wrong with this picture, Conlan, he said to himself, but he couldn't keep from studying her — and picturing their kiss.

He'd been wrong about her face, he decided. She was beautiful, with classic features, large eyes, a full mouth. He'd trailed his finger down the curve of her cheek the first time they'd met, and now he did so a second time, mentally.

She knew what he was thinking. Steve swore she did. The pulse in her throat hammered wildly and she looked away.

Steve did, too. He didn't know what was happening, didn't want to know. He reached for his beer and gulped down two deep swallows.

What on earth was he doing? Rubbing her feet, thinking about kissing her. He didn't need a woman messing up his life!

Especially a woman like Meg Remington.

"So you met Steve again," Laura said. They sat on a bench in Lincoln Park enjoying huge ice-cream cones. A ferry eased toward the dock at Fauntleroy.

"Who told you that?" Meg answered, deciding to play dumb.

"Lindsey, who else? You really didn't think you fooled her, did you?"

"No." Clearly she had no talent for subterfuge.

"So tell me how your meeting went."

Meg didn't answer. She couldn't. She wasn't sure what, if anything, she and Steve had accomplished during their meeting at the bar. They'd come up with a plan to dissuade his sister and her daughter, but the more hours that passed, the more ridiculous it seemed. And Meg's willingness, indeed her eagerness, to see Steve again was disturbing.

In retrospect she saw that it'd been a mistake for them to get together. All she could think about was how he'd lifted her legs onto his lap and rubbed the tired achiness away. There'd been a sudden explosion of awareness between them. A living, breathing, throbbing awareness.

Rarely had Meg wanted a man to kiss her more. Right in the middle of a sports bar, for heaven's sake! It was the craziest thing to happen to her in years. That of itself was distressing, but what happened afterward baffled her even more.

Melting ice cream dripped onto her hand and Meg hurriedly licked it away.

"Meg?" Laura said, studying her. "What's wrong?"

"Nothing," she said, laughing off her friend's concern. "What could possibly be wrong?"

"You haven't been yourself the last couple of days."

"Sure I have," she said, then deciding it was pointless to go on lying, she blurted out the truth. "I'm afraid I could really fall for this guy."

Laura laughed. "What's so awful about that?"

"For one thing, he isn't interested in me."

This time Laura eyed her suspiciously. "What makes you think that?"

"Several things."

Laura bit into her waffle cone. "Name one."

"Well, he wanted to meet so we could figure out a way to keep the kids from manipulating our lives."

"That sounds suspiciously like an excuse to see you again," Laura murmured.

"Trust me, it wasn't. Steve did everything but come right out and say he's not interested in me."

"You're sure about this?"

"Of course I am! There was ample opportunity for him to suggest we get to know each other better, and he didn't." She'd assumed Steve had experienced the same physical attraction she had, but maybe she'd been wrong.

Lindsey and Brenda had insisted she still had it. All Meg could say was that recent experience had proven otherwise. Whatever *it* was had long since deserted her.

"Did it occur to you that he might've been waiting for *you* to suggest something?" Laura asked.

"No," Meg told her frankly. Steve wasn't a man who took his cues from a woman. If he wanted something or someone, he'd make it known. If he wanted to continue to see her, he would've said so.

"There's got to be more than that."

"There is." Meg took a deep breath. "I was just getting ready to tell you. Steve came up with the idea originally, but I agreed."

"To what?"

Meg stood and found the closest garbage receptacle to dump what remained of her ice cream. "Before I tell you, remember I'd been drinking beer on an empty stomach." Okay, she'd had the pretzels.

"This doesn't sound promising," Laura said.

"It isn't." Drawing in another deep breath, she sat down on the park bench again. "We realized that the louder we protested and the more often we said we weren't attracted to each other, the less likely either Lindsey or Nancy will believe us."

"There's a problem with this scenario," Laura muttered.

"There is?"

"Yes. You *are* interested in Steve. Very interested." Laura gave her a look that said Meg hadn't fooled her.

Meg glanced away. "I don't want to confuse the issue with that."

"All right, go on," Laura said with a wave of her hand.

"Steve thinks the only possible way we have of convincing Lindsey that he's not the right person for me is if he starts dating me and —"

"See?" Laura said triumphantly. "He's interested. Don't you get it? This idea of his is just an excuse."

"I doubt it." Meg could see no reason for him to play games if he truly wanted a relationship with her. "You can come over this evening if you want and see for yourself."

"See what?"

"Steve's coming to meet Lindsey."

"To your house?"

"Yes."

Laura grinned widely. "R-e-a-l-l-y," she said, dragging out the word.

"Really. But it isn't what you think." Because if Laura did believe Steve wanted to pursue something with Meg, her friend was in for a major disappointment.

Meg got home an hour later. Lindsey had taken Steve's visit seriously. She'd cleaned the house, baked cookies and wore her best jeans. A dress would've been asking too much.

"Hello, sweetheart."

"Mom," Lindsey said, frowning at her watch. "Do you have any idea what time it is?"

"Yeah."

"Don't you think you should shower and change clothes? Steve will be here in an hour and a half."

"I know." She supposed she should reveal more enthusiasm, if only for show, but she couldn't make herself do it. This had been Steve's idea and she'd agreed, but she still wasn't convinced.

"I was thinking you should wear that sundress we bought last year with the pretty red-rose print," Lindsey suggested. "That and your white sandals." She studied her mother critically. "I wish you had one of those broad-brimmed sun hats. A pretty white one would be perfect. Very romantic."

"We'll just have to make do with the sombrero Grandpa bought you in Mexico," Meg teased.

"Mother," Lindsey cried, appalled. "That would look stupid!"

Meg sighed dramatically, for effect. "I don't know how I managed to dress myself all these years without you."

She thought — or hoped — that her daughter would laugh. Lindsey didn't. "That might be the reason you're still single. Have you considered that?"

This kid was no help when it came to boosting her confidence.

"You're a great mother," Lindsey said, redeeming herself somewhat, "but promise me you'll never go clothes-shopping without me again."

Rather than make rash pledges she had no intention of keeping, Meg hurried up the stairs and got into the shower. The hot water pulsating against her skin refreshed her and renewed her sense of humor. She could hardly wait to see Lindsey's face when she met Steve.

With a towel tucked around her, Meg wandered into her bedroom and examined the contents of her closet. In this case, Lindsey was right; the sundress was her best choice. She wore it, Meg told herself, because it looked good on her and *not* because Lindsey had suggested it.

Her daughter was waiting for her in the living room. The floral arrangement Steve, or rather Nancy, had sent was displayed in the middle of the coffee table.

Lindsey had polished the silver tea set until it gleamed. The previous time Meg had used it was when Pastor Delany came for a visit shortly after Meg's father died.

The doorbell chimed. Lindsey turned to her mother with a grin. "We're ready," she said, and gave her a thumbs-up sign.

Meg had assumed she knew what to expect, but when she opened the front door her mouth sagged open.

"Steve?" she whispered to the man dressed in a black leather jacket, tight blue jeans and a white T-shirt. "Is that you?"

He winked at her. "You expecting someone else?"

"N-no," she stammered.

"Invite me in," he said in a low voice. As she stepped aside, he walked past her and placed his index finger under her chin, closing her mouth.

He stood in the archway between the entry and her living room, feet braced apart. "You must be Lindsey," he said gruffly. "I'm Steve."

"You're Steve?" Lindsey sounded uncharacteristically meek.

"Lindsey, this is Steve Conlan," Meg said, standing next to him.

Steve slid his arm around Meg's waist and planted a noisy kiss on her cheek. He glanced at Lindsey. "I understand you're the one who got us together. Thanks."

"You're welcome." Lindsey's eyes didn't so much as flicker. She certainly wasn't about to let them read her thoughts. "You, uh, don't look anything like your picture."

Steve refused to take his eyes off Meg. He squeezed her waist again. "The one I sent was taken a while back," he said. "Before I went to prison."

Lindsey gasped. "Prison?"

"Don't worry, sweetheart. It wasn't a violent crime."

"What . . . were you in for?" Lindsey asked, her voice shaking.

Steve rubbed the side of his jaw, shadowed by a dark growth of beard. "If you don't mind, I'd rather not say."

"Sit down, Steve," Meg said from between gritted teeth. Talk about overkill. Any more of this and everything would be ruined.

"Would you care for coffee?" Lindsey asked. Her young voice continued to tremble.

"You got a beer?"

"It's not a good idea to be drinking this early in the afternoon, is it?" Meg asked sweetly.

Steve sat down on the sofa, balancing his ankle on the opposite knee. He looked around as if he were casing the joint.

Meg moved to the silver service. "Coffee or tea?"

"Coffee, but add a little something that'll give it some kick."

Meg poured coffee for him and added a generous dollop of half-and-half. He frowned at the delicate bone china cup as though he wasn't sure how to hold it.

Lindsey sat down on the ottoman, her eyes huge. "I . . . you never said anything about prison."

"Don't like to mention it until people have a chance to meet me for themselves. Some of 'em tend to think the worst of a person when they hear he's had a felony conviction."

"A . . . felony." Lindsey snapped her mouth shut, inhaled deeply, then said in a subdued tone, "I see."

"The flowers are lovely." Meg fingered a rosebud from the bouquet.

Steve grinned. "My probation officer told me women like that sort of thing. Glad to know he was right." He sipped his coffee and made a slurping sound. "By the way, you'll be glad to hear I told him about you and me, and he did a background check on you and said it was fine for us to see each other."

"That's wonderful," Meg said with enthu-

77

siasm that wasn't *entirely* faked.

Steve set aside the delicate cup and leaned forward, his elbows on his knees. He stared at Lindsey and smiled. "Yup, I got to thank you," he said. "I realize your mother's upset with you placing that ad and everything. It's usually not a good idea to fool someone like that, but I wasn't being completely honest with you, either, so I guess we're even."

Lindsey nodded.

"Your mother's one special woman. There aren't a lot of females who'd be willing to overlook my past. Most women don't care that I've got a heart of gold. Your mama did. We sat down in that fancy restaurant and I took one look at her pretty face and I knew she was the woman for me." He rubbed the side of his unshaven jaw and laughed. "I do have to tell you, though, that when you suggested Chez Michelle, I was afraid Meg might be too high maintenance for someone like me."

"I'm sorry . . ." Lindsey floundered with the apology. "I didn't know."

"Don't you worry. Your mama was worth every penny of that fancy dinner. Just getting to know her and love her — why, a man couldn't ask for a prettier gal." He eyed her as if she were a Thanksgiving feast, then moistened his lips, implying it was all he could do to keep from grabbing her right then and there and kissing her.

"Steve . . ." Meg muttered.

"Sorry," he said, and seemed to pull himself together. "Earl Markham, my probation officer, says I've gotta be careful not to rush things. But I look at your beautiful eyes and I can't help myself."

"Yes, well . . ."

"You didn't tell me how good-looking your daughter is," he said, as though Meg had purposely been holding out on him.

"Lindsey's my pride and joy," Meg said, beaming her daughter a smile.

"I got plenty of friends who wouldn't mind meeting a good-looking girl like you." He winked at Lindsey, suggesting that all he needed was one word from her and he'd make the arrangements immediately.

"Absolutely not!" Meg said, forgetting this was just a game. "I won't have you introducing my daughter to your friends."

Steve's eyes widened with surprise and he held up his right hand, as if taking an oath. "Sorry, I didn't mean to offend. You don't want Lindsey dating any of my buddies, fine, I'll see it never happens."

"Good." Meg had to acknowledge that Steve was an excellent actor. He almost had *her* believing him. She suspected that was because he'd turned himself into the man she'd half expected to meet that night.

Steve smacked his lips. "I gotta tell you when I first saw Meg in that pretty black dress, my heart went all the way to the floor. She's the most beautiful woman I've seen since I was released." His eyes softened as his gaze fell on Meg.

"Released?" Lindsey squeaked.

"From prison," Steve clarified, his gaze immediately returning to Meg.

It would help considerably if he didn't look so sincere, Meg thought.

"Yes, well . . ." she said, standing. But once she was on her feet, she wasn't sure what to do.

"I'll bet you want me to take you on that motorcycle ride I been promising you," Steve said, downing the last of his coffee.

"Mom's going on a motorcycle with you?" Lindsey asked, swallowing visibly.

"I'd better change clothes," Meg said, eager to escape so she could speak to Steve alone.

"No need," Steve said. "You can ride sidesaddle if you want. I brought my Hog. There's plenty of room, although I gotta tell you, I been dreaming about you sitting behind me, wrapping your arms around my waist. You'll need to hold on tight, honey, real tight." His eyes didn't waver from hers, and the sexual innuendo was unmistakable.

"Yes, well . . ." Either the room had grown considerably warmer or Meg was in deep trouble.

Judging by the look of disgust Lindsey cast her, she could see it was the latter.

"I think I'll change into a pair of jeans, if it's all the same to you."

"Sure," Steve said, wiping the back of his hand across his mouth. "Just don't keep me waiting long, you hear?"

"I won't," she promised.

Meg rushed toward the stairs, anxious to get away.

Steve reached out to stop her. His hand closed over her shoulder and he brought her into his arms. She gasped in shock. Without giving her time to recover, he lowered his mouth to hers.

It was all for show, but that didn't keep her heart from fluttering wildly. Her stomach muscles tightened at the unexpectedness of his kiss.

Her lips parted and she slid her arms tightly around his narrow waist.

Steve groaned and Meg was afraid the hunger she felt in him was a reflection of her own. By the time he dragged his lips from hers they were both panting. Speechless, they stared at each other.

"I'll . . . I'll be right back," she managed to whisper. Then she raced up the stairs as if demons were in hot pursuit. On the way she caught a glimpse of Lindsey staring after her, open-mouthed.

FOUR

The minute they were alone outside, Meg hit Steve across his upper arm, hurting her hand in the process. Biting her lip, she shook her fingers several times, then clutched her aching hand protectively with the other.

"What was that for?" Steve demanded, glaring at her.

"You overdid it," she snapped, barely understanding her own outrage.

"I had to convince her I was unsuitable, didn't I?"

Meg bristled. "Yes, but you went above and beyond what we discussed. All that business about me being so beautiful," she muttered as she walked to the driveway where he'd parked the Harley-Davidson. She climbed onto the leather seat without thinking.

"I thought I did a great job," Steve argued. A smile raised the edges of his mouth.

"That's another thing," she said, unable to stop looking at him. "Was that kiss really necessary?"

"Yes," he said calmly, but Meg could tell that he didn't take kindly to her rebuke. "Lindsey needed to see me in action," he insisted.

"You frightened my daughter half out of her wits as it was. There was no need to . . ."

Steve's eyes widened, then softened into a smile. "You liked the kiss," he said flatly. "You liked it and that scared you."

"Don't be ridiculous! It . . . it was disgusting."

"No, it wasn't." His smile was cocky. He laughed, the timbre low and mildly threatening. "Maybe I should prove how wrong you are."

Meg shifted uncomfortably on the seat. "Let's get this over with," she said, feigning boredom. "You're going to take me out for an hour or so and then drive me back. Right? By the way, where did you get the motorcycle?"

He advanced a step toward her. "It's mine."

"Yours?" He was exactly the kind of man her mother had warned her about, and here she was flirting with danger. He moved a step closer and she held herself rigid.

"You don't know much about men, do you?" he asked, his voice low and husky.

"I was married for nearly six years," she informed him primly. He was close now, too close. She kept her spine stiff and her eyes straight ahead. If the motorcycle was his, it was reasonable to assume the leather jacket belonged to him as well. The persona he'd taken on, the criminal element, might not be too far from the truth.

"You haven't been with a man since, have you?"

She felt his breath against her flushed face. "I refuse to answer questions of a personal nature," she returned, her voice hoarse and low.

"You haven't," he said confidently. "Look at me, Meg."

"No. Let's get this ride over with."

"Look at me," he repeated.

She tried to resist, but the words were warm and hypnotic. Against her better judgment, she twisted toward him. "Yes?" she asked, her heart pounding so hard she thought it might leap right through her chest.

He wove his hands into her hair and tilted her head back so that she couldn't avoid staring up at him. His gaze bored relentlessly into hers.

"Admit it," he whispered. "You enjoyed the kiss." His eyes were compelling, she admitted reluctantly, resisting him every step.

"How like a man — everything's about ego," she said in an effort to make light of what had happened. "Even a silly little kiss."

Steve frowned.

There was a fluttery feeling in the pit of her stomach, the same feeling that had attacked her when he'd kissed her by the staircase. She felt vulnerable and helpless.

"It wasn't little and it wasn't silly. But it was what we both wanted," he said in a deceptively normal voice.

"You're crazy," she murmured, hurrying to assure him that he'd been wrong. Very wrong. She lowered her eyes, but this proved to be a tactical error. Before she realized what he intended, he was kissing her again.

Meg wanted to protest. If she'd fought him, struggled, he might have released her. But her one weak objection came in the form of a moan, and it appeared to encourage rather than dissuade him.

All at once it was important to get closer. A moment later she was kneeling on the leather cushion and Steve had slipped his arms around her middle. They didn't stay there long. He glided his hands along her back, urging her more tightly against him.

Meg didn't require much inducement. Her body willfully molded itself to his. Then, abruptly, her eyes fluttered open and with a determined effort she broke free. Steve's arms tightened before he relaxed and finally released her.

The look on his face was one of shock.

For her own part, Meg was having a difficult time breathing. Sensations swarmed through her. Unwanted sensations. Steve made her feel as if she'd never been kissed before, never been held or loved. Never been married or shared intimacies with a man.

She blinked, and Steve backed away. He frowned and raked his fingers through his hair, apparently sorting out his own troubled emotions.

"I suppose you expect me to admit I enjoyed that," she said with more than a hint of belligerence. These feelings frightened her. The fact that she'd reacted to him could easily be explained. Good grief, she was a normal woman — but this giddy, end-of-the-world sensation wasn't anything she'd ever experienced.

"You don't have to admit to a damned thing," he said. He climbed onto the Hog and revved the engine aggressively.

"Stop," she cried, shouting above the noise. She waved a hand to clear away the exhaust.

"What's wrong now?" he snapped, twisting around to look at her.

"Nothing. . . . Just go slow, all right?"

Separated by only a couple of inches, Meg felt him tense. "I'm not exactly in a slow mood."

"I guessed as much."

She didn't know what he intended as he expertly maneuvered the motorcycle out of her driveway. Mortified, Meg glanced up and down the street, wondering how many of her neighbors had witnessed the exchange between her and Steve. Fortunately Lindsey wasn't at the front window watching as Meg had half feared.

"Hang on," he shouted.

She placed her hands lightly on either side of his waist, hoping to keep the contact as impersonal as possible — until they turned the first corner. From that moment on, she wrapped her arms around him as tightly as she could.

Meg was grateful that he chose not to drive far. He stopped at a park less than a mile from her house. After he'd eased into a parking space, he switched off the engine and sat motionless for a couple of minutes.

"You okay?" he asked after a while.

"I'm fine. Great. That was . . . fun." She was astonished at her new talent for telling white lies. She was far from fine. Her insides were a mess, although that had almost nothing to do with the motorcycle ride. Her heart refused to settle down to a normal pace, and she couldn't stop thinking about their kisses. The first time had been traumatic, but it didn't compare to her nearly suffocating reaction to his second kiss.

Steve checked his watch. "We'll give it another five minutes and then I'll take you back to the house. That should give Lindsey enough time to worry about you without sending her into a panic."

"Perfect," she said brightly — a little too brightly.

"Then tomorrow afternoon I'll pick you up after work and you can do your thing with my sister."

Although he couldn't see her, she nodded. Meg only hoped her act for Nancy would be as convincing as Steve's had been with Lindsey.

"After that, we won't need to see each other again," Steve said. "As far as I'm concerned, it isn't a minute too soon."

Meg felt much the same way. She was just

89

as eager to get him out of her life.

Wasn't she?

It hadn't been a good day. Steve would've liked to blame his foul mood on work-related problems, but everything at Emerald City Body Shop had run like clockwork. The one reason that presented itself was Meg Remington.

He'd known from the first night that getting involved with her would mean trouble. Sure enough, he was waist-deep in quicksand, and all because he hadn't wanted to hurt the woman's feelings.

Okay, that accounted for their dinner date, but afterward . . . what happened was no one's fault except his own. Donning his leather jacket and jeans and playing the role of the disgruntled ex-con had been fun. But then he had to go and do something stupid.

The stupid part was because of the kiss. He'd been a fool to force Meg to admit how good it had been. This was what he got for allowing his pride to stand in the way.

Well, Steve had learned his lesson. The next time he was tempted to kiss Meg, he'd go stand in the middle of the freeway. Man, oh man, she could kiss. Only she didn't seem to realize it. Much more of that kissing and he would've been renting a hotel room.

Not Meg, though. Oh, no. She acted as outraged as a nun. Apparently she'd forgotten that men and women did that sort of thing. Enjoyed it, too. Looked forward to doing it again.

The woman was insane, and the sooner he could extract her from his life, the better. He didn't need this. Who did?

One more night, he assured himself. He was taking Meg to meet Nancy this evening, and when they were finished, it would be over and they'd never have to see each other again. If she played her cards right. He'd done his part.

Despite his sour mood, Steve grinned. He'd never forget the look of shock and horror in Lindsey's eyes when he walked into the house. Her jaw had nearly hit the carpet when he put his arms around Meg's waist and announced that he was an ex-con. He wouldn't forget the look in Meg's eyes, either.

Steve laughed outright.

"Something funny?" Gary Wilcox asked.

Steve glared at his foreman. "Not a thing. Now get back to work."

At six o'clock, Steve pulled into the parking space in the alley behind Meg's bookstore. He didn't like the idea of sneaking around and going to her back door, but that was what Meg wanted and far be it from him to argue. He'd be well rid of the woman — at least that was what he kept trying to tell himself.

He knocked and waited a few minutes, growing impatient.

The door opened and a woman in black mesh nylons and the shortest miniskirt he'd seen in years stood in front of him. She vaguely resembled Tina Turner. She wore tons of makeup and she'd certainly had her hair done at the same salon as Tina.

"I'm here for Meg Remington," he said, annoyed that Meg had made such a fuss about his coming to the back door and then sent someone else to answer it.

"Steve," Meg whispered, "it's me."

"What the hell?" He jerked his head back and examined her more thoroughly. "We're meeting my sister," he reminded her stiffly, "not going to some costume party."

"I took my cue from you," she said. "Good grief! You arrived at my door looking like a Hell's Angel — what did you expect *me* to do?"

Steve rubbed his face. Darned if he knew anymore. All he wanted was to get this over with. "Fine. Let's get out of here."

"Just a minute. I need to change shoes."

She slipped out of a perfectly fine pair of flats and into spiky high heels that added a good five inches to her height. Steve wondered how she'd manage to walk in those things. She might as well have been on stilts.

He led her around to his car and opened the door. He noticed that she sighed with what sounded like relief once she was inside the car.

"I didn't know what I was going to do if you brought that motorcycle again." She tugged down her miniskirt self-consciously.

"For the record, I don't often take it out."

She looked relieved, but why it should matter to her one way or the other, he had no idea.

"Just remember," he said, feeling obliged to caution her. "Nancy's a few years older than Lindsey. She won't be as easily fooled."

"I'll be careful about overkill," she mumbled, "unlike certain people I know."

The drive took an eternity, and it wasn't due to heavy traffic, either. In fact, when Steve looked at his watch he was surprised at what good time they'd made. What made the drive so troublesome — he hated to admit this — was Meg's legs. She'd crossed them, exposing plenty of smooth, shapely thigh. Her high heels dangled from the ends of her toes.

Steve appreciated women as a whole — some more than others, of course. He didn't focus on body parts. But it was torture to sit with Meg in the close confines of his car and keep his eyes off her legs. The woman looked incredible. If only she'd keep her mouth shut!

Nancy was standing on the porch when Steve pulled into the driveway.

"This is where your sister lives?" Meg asked.

"It's my home," Steve answered, certain she was about to find something wrong with it.

"Your home?" She sounded impressed. "It's very nice."

"Thanks." He turned off the engine. "Nancy's quite a bit younger than I am — a surprise for my mom and dad. She attends college at the University of Washington nine months out of the year. Our parents retired to Montana a couple of years back."

"I see. Does Nancy live with you?"

"Not on your life," he said, climbing out of the car. "She's in residence during the school year. She got a job here this summer and I agreed to let her stay with me a few months. A mistake I don't plan to repeat anytime soon."

Steve was watching for his sister's reaction when he helped Meg out of the car. To her credit, the nineteen-year-old didn't reveal much, but Steve knew her well enough to realize she was shocked by Meg's appearance.

"You must be Nancy," Meg said in a low, sultry voice.

"And you must be Meg," Nancy said, coming down the steps to greet her. "I've been dying to meet you."

"I hope I'm not a disappointment." This was said in a soft, cooing tone, as if she couldn't have tolerated disillusioning Steve's little sister. She clasped Steve's arm and he noticed for the first time that her nails — now two inches long — were painted a brilliant fire engine red.

Nancy held open the door and smiled in welcome. "Please, come inside."

Meg's high heels clattered against the tile entryway. Steve looked around, pleased to note that his sister had cleaned up the house a bit.

"Oh, Stevie," Meg whined, "you never told me what a beautiful home you have." She trailed one finger along the underside of his jaw. "But then, we haven't had time to discuss much of anything, have we?"

"Make yourself comfortable," Steve said

and watched as Meg chose to sit on the sofa. She sat, crossing her legs with great ceremony. Then she patted the empty space beside her, silently requesting Steve to join her there. He glanced longingly at his favorite chair, but moved across the room and sat down next to Meg.

The minute he was comfortable, Meg placed her hand possessively on his knee and flexed her nails into his thigh. Inch by provocative inch she raked her nails up his leg until it was all Steve could do not to pop straight off the sofa. He caught her hand and stopped her from reaching what seemed to be her ultimate destination.

Her expression was mildly repentant when she looked at him, but Steve knew her well enough to know the action had been deliberate.

"I thought you might be hungry before Steve takes you to dinner, so I made a few hors d'oeuvres," Nancy said and excused herself.

"What are you doing?" Steve whispered the minute his sister was out of the room.

"Doing? What do you mean?" She had wide-eyed innocence down to an art.

"Never mind," he muttered as Nancy returned from the kitchen carrying a small silver platter.

"Those look wonderful," Meg said sweetly when his sister put the tray on the coffee table in front of them. "But I couldn't eat a thing."

To the best of his knowledge it was the first time his sister had cooked from the moment she'd moved in with him, and he wasn't about to let it go to waste. He chose a tiny wiener wrapped in some kind of crispy dough and tossed it in his mouth.

"You shouldn't have gone to all this trouble," Meg told his sister.

Nancy sat across the room from them, apparently at a complete loss for words.

"I suspect you're wondering about all these letters and e-mails I wrote," Meg said, getting the conversation going. "I hope you aren't unhappy with me."

"No, no, not at all," Nancy said, rushing the words together.

"It's just that I've come to know what people *really* want from me by the things they say." She turned, and with the tip of her index finger wiped a crumb from the corner of his mouth. Her tongue moistened her lips and Steve's insides turned to mush.

"I learned a long time ago what men want from a woman," Meg continued after a moment, "especially when I went to work for a phone sex line. Most of the guys are just looking for a woman to talk dirty to them."

"I see." Nancy folded her hands primly in her lap.

"There was the occasional guy who was looking for a good girl to shock, of course. I got very talented at acting horrified." She made a soft, gasping sound, then laughed demurely.

"Why . . . why would someone like you place an ad in Dateline?" Nancy asked, nervously brushing the hair from her face.

"Well, first," Meg said, holding his sister's gaze, "it's just about the only way someone like me can meet anyone decent. But it wasn't your brother who answered the ad, now, was it?"

"No, but —"

"Not that it matters," Meg said, cutting her off. "I was tired of my job and all those guys asking me to say those nasty things, and I didn't want to start working on my back again."

"On your . . . back," Nancy repeated.

"I'm sorry, sugar. I didn't mean to shock you. I've got a colorful past — but that doesn't mean I'm a bad girl. I've got a heart just brimming with love. All I need is the right man." Her gaze wandered to Steve and was long and deliberate. "Your brother's given me a reason to dream again," Meg said softly. "Lots of people think women like me don't have feelings, but they're wrong."

"I'm sure that's true," Nancy said tentatively.

"I knew I chose right when I found out your brother has his own business."

"He's struggled financially for years," Nancy was quick to tell her. "It's still touch and go. He lives from one month to the next." Nancy glared at him pointedly. "Don't you, Steve?"

"Not anymore. I'm more than solvent now," Steve tossed in for good measure, struggling not to laugh. He was enjoying this.

Meg tightened her arm around his. "I can see how well Stevie's doing for himself. He's wonderful," she said, refusing to look away. The adoration on her face embarrassed him.

"Why, Steve here could make enough money to keep me in the lifestyle to which I'd like to become accustomed." She laughed coyly.

"Ah . . ." It sounded to Steve as if his sister was close to hyperventilating.

"Of course, I wouldn't take anything from him without giving in return. That wouldn't be fair." She snuggled closer to his side and gave him a look so purely sexual Steve was convinced he'd embarrass them all.

"There are things I could teach your brother," Meg said in a husky voice full of sexual innuendo. She acted as though she was eager to get started right that moment and the only thing holding her back was propriety. Her breathing grew heavy — and if he didn't know better he'd think she actually *had* worked for one of those disreputable phone services.

Soon he was having a problem controlling his own breathing.

"Steve!" Nancy snapped.

He turned his attention back to his sister, staring at her blankly.

"Didn't you hear Meg?" she asked.

He shrugged. He knew the two women were talking, but he'd barely noticed their conversation.

"Meg's talking about moving in with you," Nancy said through clenched teeth.

"I don't mean to rush you, darlin'," Meg whispered. Leaning forward, she licked his earlobe with the tip of her tongue.

Hot sensation shot down his spine.

Meg threw back her head and laughed softly, then whispered just loudly enough for Nancy to hear, "I have an incredibly talented tongue."

Nancy closed her eyes as if she couldn't

bear to watch another minute of this. Frankly, Steve didn't know how much more he could take himself.

"I think it's time we left for dinner," he said. Otherwise he was going to start believing all the promises Meg was making. Heaven knew, he *wanted* to believe them. The demure bookseller had turned into something completely different. All traces of innocence had disappeared and in their place was the most sexually provocative female he'd ever met. Just being in the same room with her made his blood sizzle.

"You want to leave already?" Meg gave the impression that she was terribly disappointed.

"That's probably best," Nancy muttered, and then realizing what she'd said, hurried to add, "I mean, you two don't want to waste your evening with me, do you?" She frowned at Steve. "You won't be late, will you?"

"No."

"Unfortunately, I'm still working for the phone people," Meg said, "so I won't keep him too long, but I can't promise he'll have much kick left in him when I'm finished." Apparently thinking herself exceptionally clever, Meg laughed at her own joke.

It wasn't until they were back in the car

and on the freeway that Steve recognized how angry he was. It made no sense, but he wasn't exactly rational just then.

"Why are you so mad?" Meg asked about halfway back to the bookstore. They hadn't spoken a word from the time they'd left his house.

"Talk about overkill," he muttered.

"I thought I did a good job," she said.

"You came off like a —"

"I know. That's what I wanted. After meeting me, do you honestly think your sister's going to encourage our relationship?"

"No," he growled.

"I can guarantee you that Lindsey doesn't want me to see you, either. I thought that's what this whole scheme of yours was about."

"It sounded like a good idea at the time." He tightened his hands on the steering wheel. "It seemed like a surefire way to convince your daughter that I was the wrong man for you."

"And your sister that I was equally wrong for you."

Silence settled over them like nightfall. Neither of them seemed inclined to talk again.

Steve edged his car into the alley behind Meg's store and parked his car behind hers.

"I'm not so sure anymore," he said without looking at her.

"About what?"

"The two of us. Somewhere in the middle of all this, I decided I kind of like you." It hadn't been easy to admit, and he hoped she appreciated what it had cost his pride. "It probably wouldn't have been as obvious if you hadn't made yourself out to be so cheap. That isn't you any more than the rebel without a cause is me."

He wished she'd say something. When she did speak, her voice was timid and small. "Then there was the kiss."

"Kisses," he corrected. "They were pretty great and we both know it," he said with confidence. He knew what his own reaction had been, and she hadn't fooled him with hers.

"Yes," she said softly.

"Especially the one on the motorcycle," he said, prompting her to continue.

"Especially the one on the motorcycle," she mimicked. "Honestly, Steve, you must've known."

His smile was full blown. "I did."

"I . . . I didn't do a very good job of disguising what I was feeling."

She hadn't, but he was in a gracious mood.

"How about dinner?" he suggested. He

was eager to have the real Meg Remington back. Eager to experiment with a few more kisses — see if they were anything close to what his memory kept insisting they'd been.

She hesitated. "I want to, but I can't," she eventually said.

He bristled and turned in the driver's seat to face her. "Why not?"

"I promised Lindsey I'd be home by seven and it's nearly that now."

"Call her and tell her you're going out to dinner with me."

She dragged in a deep breath and seemed to hold it. "I can't do that, either."

"Why not?"

"After meeting you, I promised her we'd talk. She wanted to last evening, and we didn't. . . . That was my fault. You kissed me," she said, "and I didn't feel like a heart-to-heart with my daughter after that."

"And it's all my fault?"

"Yes," she insisted.

"Do you know what Lindsey wants to discuss?"

"Of course, I know. You. She doesn't want me seeing you again, which is exactly the point of the entire charade. Remember?"

"Yeah," Steve said, scowling.

"Are . . . are you telling me you've changed your mind?" she asked.

"Yes." He hated to be the one to say it first, but one of them had to. "What about you?"

"I think so."

Steve flattened his hand against the steering wheel. "I swear you're about the worst thing that's ever happened to my ego."

She laughed and rested her hand on his shoulder. The wig she had on tilted sideways and she righted it. "That does sound terrible, doesn't it?"

He smiled. "Yeah. The least you could do is show some enthusiasm."

"I haven't dated much in the last ten years. But if I was going to choose any man, it would be you."

"That's better," he said. He wanted to kiss her. He'd been thinking about it from the moment he'd picked her up.

"Only . . ." Meg said sadly.

"Only what?" he repeated, lowering his mouth to hers.

Their lips met and it was heaven, just the way he'd known it would be. By the time the kiss ended, Steve was leaning his head against the window of the car door, his eyes closed. It was even more wonderful than he'd remembered, and that seemed impossible.

Meg's head was on his chest, tucked

beneath his chin.

"It's too late," she whispered.

"What's too late?"

"We've gone to all this trouble to convince Lindsey that you're all wrong for me."

"I know, but . . ."

"Do you think Nancy will believe this was all a silly joke?"

"No."

"I think we should end everything right here and now, don't you?" she asked.

Steve stiffened. "If that's what you want."

She moved away from him. "I guess it is," she said, with just a hint of regret.

FIVE

Lindsey was pacing the living room, waiting for Meg when she walked in the front door.

"Hi, honey," Meg said, trying to sound cheerful yet exhausted — since she'd led Lindsey to believe she was taking inventory at the bookstore and that was why she'd come home so late.

"It's way after seven!" her daughter cried, rushing toward her. "You weren't with Steve, were you?"

"Ah . . ." Meg wasn't willing to lie outright. Half truths and innuendos were about as far as she wanted to stretch this.

Lindsey closed her eyes and waved her hands vaguely. "Forget it. Don't answer that."

"Honey, what's wrong?" Meg asked as calmly as she could. Unfortunately, she didn't think she sounded all that reassuring. She'd left Steve only moments earlier and was already feeling some regret. After following through with this ridiculous charade, Steve wanted to change his mind and continue seeing Meg. She'd quickly put an end to *that* idea. Now she wasn't sure she'd made the right decision.

"Mom," Lindsey said, her dark eyes challenging, "we need to talk."

"Of course." Meg walked into the kitchen and took the china teapot from the hutch. "My mother always made tea when we had something to discuss." Somehow, the ritual of drinking tea together put everything in perspective. Meg missed those times with her mother.

Lindsey helped her assemble everything they needed and carried it into the dining room. Meg poured them each a cup, once the tea had steeped, and they sat across from each other at the polished mahogany table.

Meg waited, and when Lindsey wasn't immediately forthcoming she decided to get the conversation started. "You wanted to talk to me about Steve, right?"

Lindsey clasped the delicate china cup with one hand and lowered her gaze. "Do you really, really like him?" she asked anxiously.

Meg answered before she took time to censor the question. "Yes."

"But why? I mean, he's nothing like what I thought he'd be." She hesitated. "I suppose this is what Brenda and I get for pretending we were you," she mumbled. "Maybe if you'd read his stuff, you would've been able to tell what kind of guy he really is."

"Steve is actually a fine person." And he was. Or at least the Steve Meg knew.

Lindsey risked a glance at her. "You've said hundreds of times that you don't want me to judge others by outward appearances, but sometimes that's all there is."

"You're worried about me and Steve, aren't you?" Meg said gently.

Lindsey rubbed her finger along the edge of the teacup. "I realize now that what Brenda and I did was really stupid. We linked you up with a guy who has a prison record. We sure were easy to fool," Lindsey said with a scowl. "We're only fifteen years old!"

"But I like Steve," Meg felt obliged to tell her.

Lindsey looked as if she didn't know how to account for that. "I'm afraid he's going to hurt you."

"Steve wouldn't do that," Meg assured her, "but I understand your concern, honey, and I promise you I won't let the situation get out of hand."

Lindsey frowned, stiffened her shoulders and blurted out, "I don't want you to see him again."

"But . . ."

"I mean it, Mom. This guy is trouble."

Talk about role reversal!

"I want you to *promise* me you won't see Steve Conlan again."

"Lindsey . . ."

"This is important. You may not understand it now, but I promise you will in the future. There are plenty of other men, law-abiding citizens, who'd give their right arms to meet a woman like you."

Meg stared. She couldn't be hearing this. This sounded exactly like something her mother had said back when Meg was in high school.

The intense look in Lindsey's eyes softened and she gestured weakly. "The time will come when you'll thank me for this."

"Really?" Meg couldn't resist raising her eyebrows.

"There'll be a boy in my life that you'll disapprove of and I won't understand why," Lindsey went on. "When that happens, I want you to remind me of now."

Meg shook her head — in bafflement and disbelief. "Are you telling me you'd break up with a boy simply because I didn't like him?"

"No," Lindsey said carefully. "But I'd consider it because I know how I feel about you seeing Steve, and I'd understand how you might feel about someone I was dating. Don't get me wrong," she hurried to add, "I don't dislike Steve. . . . He's kind of cute. It's just that I feel you could do a whole lot better."

"I'll think about it," Meg promised.

Lindsey nodded. "I can't ask for more than that."

Her daughter had behaved just as Meg had predicted. This had gone precisely according to plan. But Meg didn't feel good about it. If anything, she felt more depressed following their conversation than before.

She didn't have any talent when it came to relationships, Meg decided, as she finished putting away the dinner dishes later that evening. Steve had come right out and told her he'd had a change of heart, and she'd bungled everything. Instead of admitting that she felt the same way he did, she'd trampled all over his ego.

Meg turned to the kitchen phone, tempted to call him. It couldn't end like this, with such confusion, such uncertainty about what she really wanted. What *they* wanted.

111

Never had an evening passed more slowly. It seemed to take Lindsey hours to go to bed, and by then Meg was yawning herself.

As soon as Meg could be reasonably sure that her daughter was asleep, she tiptoed toward the kitchen phone and dialed Steve's number, her heart pounding. Finally she heard his groggy voice.

"Steve?" she whispered. "Thank goodness it's you. I didn't know what I was going to do if Nancy answered."

"Meg? Is that you?" He sounded surprised to hear from her, and none too pleased.

She bristled. "How many other women do you have phoning you at eleven o'clock at night?"

He didn't respond right away, and when he spoke his voice definitely lacked welcome. "I thought you said it wasn't a good idea for us to see each other."

"I . . . I don't know what I want."

"Do you expect me to make your decisions for you?"

"Of course not." This wasn't going well. In fact, it was going very badly. She probably should've waited until she'd had time to figure this out a little more clearly.

"Is there a reason you called?" he asked gruffly.

"Yes," she said, sorry now that she'd

phoned him. "I wanted to apologize for being abrupt earlier. I . . . can see now that I shouldn't have called."

Having said that, she carefully replaced the receiver. For a long moment she stared at the phone, feeling like an idiot.

She'd turned away to head up the stairs when the phone rang, jolting her. Quickly she grabbed it before the noise could wake Lindsey.

"Hello," she whispered.

"Meet me." It was Steve.

"I can't leave Lindsey."

"Why not? She's in bed, isn't she?"

"Yes, but . . ."

"Write her a note. Tell her you're going to the grocery store."

How reasonable he made it sound — as if she usually did her shopping in the middle of the night.

"She won't even know you're gone," Steve said.

Meg closed her eyes. They'd been together only a few hours earlier, and yet it felt as if they'd been apart for weeks.

Her stomach twisted. Then — before she could change her mind — she blurted out, "All right, but I can't stay long."

"Fair enough."

They agreed to meet in the Albertson's

parking lot. The huge store was open twenty-four hours a day. Meg had been shopping there for years. The note she left Lindsey said she'd gone to pick up some milk — that classic excuse — but it was exactly what she intended to do.

She sat in her car until she saw Steve pull into the nearly empty lot. Uncertain she was doing the right thing, she got out and waited for him.

Steve parked in the spot next to hers. They stood facing each other for a moment, neither speaking.

"I can't believe we're doing this," she said.

It appeared she wasn't the only one with doubts. Steve's face was blank, emotionless. "Me neither."

They walked into the store together and reached for grocery carts. Meg's had a squeaky wheel. The sound echoed through the cavernous store.

The deli was closed, but Steve was able to get them each a cup of coffee from the friendly night manager. They parked their empty carts and sat at a small white table in the deli section. Neither seemed inclined to speak.

She felt encouraged that Steve had phoned her back, but she suspected he regretted it now.

"You know what you said earlier?" she began.

"I said lots of things earlier. Which particular thing are you referring to?"

Meg guessed his sarcasm was warranted. After all, she'd wounded his ego, and he wasn't giving her the chance to do it again. "About the two of us, you know, dating."

"You said Lindsey wouldn't like it."

"She doesn't," Meg said. "She asked me not to see you again."

His gaze pinned hers. "Did you agree?"

"Not . . . entirely."

His eyes narrowed with a frown. "You'd better explain."

"Well, as you've already surmised, Lindsey isn't keen on me seeing you. Which is exactly the reason you stopped by the house and did your biker routine, right? Well, it worked. She's worried that you're the wrong man for me." It would've helped if he hadn't bragged about his prison record and mentioned his parole officer's name. But now didn't seem to be the time to bring that up.

"Did you or did you not promise her you wouldn't see me again?"

"Neither." Meg sipped from the disposable cup and grimaced at the taste of burned coffee.

"Then what *did* you say to her?"

Meg lifted one shoulder in a shrug. "That I'd think about it."

"Have you?"

Propping her elbows on the table's edge, Meg swirled the black liquid around the cup and avoided looking at Steve. "I called you, didn't I?"

"I still haven't figured out why."

That was the problem: she hadn't, either. Not really. "I guess it's because you have a point about seeing each other again."

"Oh, yeah?" He gave her a cocky grin.

Her anger flared. "Would you stop it?"

"Stop what?" he asked innocently.

"The next thing I know, you're going to ask me how much I enjoyed kissing you."

Steve smiled for the first time. "It wouldn't hurt to know."

"All right, since it means so much to you, I'll admit it. No man's ever kissed me the way you do. It scares me — but at the same time I wish it could go on forever." Having admitted this much, she supposed she might as well say it all. "My marriage left me wondering if I was . . . if I was capable of those kinds of feelings. . . ." She paused and lowered her eyes. "I was afraid I was, you know, frigid," she said in a choked whisper.

She stared down at her coffee, then took a sip, followed by several more, as if the vile stuff were the antidote to some dreaded illness.

The last thing she expected her small confession to provoke in Steve was a laugh. "You're joking!"

She shook her head forcefully. "Don't laugh. Please."

His hand reached for hers and their fingers entwined. "I wasn't laughing at you, Meg," he said gently. "You're one of the most sensual women I've ever met. Trust me, if you're frigid — and there's a word I haven't heard in years — then I'm a monk."

Meg looked up and offered him a fragile smile. It astonished her that this man who'd known her for only a few days could chase away the doubts that had hounded her through the years after her divorce.

He cleared his throat. "I, uh, don't think you should look at me like that."

"Like what?"

"Like you want me to kiss you."

Her eyes drifted shut. "Maybe I do. . . . That's what makes everything so complicated. I'm really attracted to you. I haven't felt like this before — not ever, not even with my ex-husband, and like I said, that scares me."

He stood up, still holding Meg's hand, and tugged her to her feet.

"Where are we going?" she asked.

"Someplace private," he said, scanning the store. He led her through the frozen food section, past the bakery and into a small alcove where the wine was kept. With her back to the domestic beer, he brought her into his arms and covered her mouth with his.

Their kiss was rough with need, but she wasn't sure whose need was greater. Meg could feel Steve's heart racing as hard as her own. She supposed she should've pulled away, ended the kiss, stepped out of his arms. But Meg didn't want that.

Steve yawned. He was *so* tired. With good reason. It'd been almost three before he'd gone to bed and four before he'd been able to fall asleep. His alarm had gone off at six.

He arrived at the shop and made a pot of coffee. He mumbled a greeting when Gary got in.

"I hope you're in a better mood than you were yesterday," his foreman told him. "What's wrong with you, anyway?"

Steve checked over the job orders for the day. "Women," he muttered in explanation and apology.

"I should've guessed. What's going on?"

"You don't want to hear this," he said and

118

headed for the garage.

"Sure I do," Gary said, following him. "I don't suppose this has anything to do with Nancy, does it?"

Steve glared at him. "What do you know about my sister?"

"Not much," Gary said and held up both hands. "Just what you said about her fixing you up with some woman. It's none of my business, but you and this woman seem to be hitting it off just fine."

Steve continued to glare at him. "What makes you say that?"

Gary laughed. "I haven't seen you this miserable in years. Which probably means you've fallen for her. Why don't you put yourself out of your misery? Shoot yourself and be done with it."

Frowning, Steve turned away. The kid was a smartass, although now that Steve thought about it, Gary might have come up with the perfect solution.

It was noon before Steve had a chance to go into his office. He made sure no one was looking, then closed the door and reached for the phone.

"Book Ends, Laura speaking," a woman said in a friendly voice.

"Is Meg available?" he asked, sounding as

119

businesslike as possible.

"May I ask who's calling?"

Steve hesitated. "Steve Conlan."

"One minute, please."

It took longer than that for Meg to get on the line. "Steve, hi." She seemed tired but happy to hear from him. That helped.

"How are you?" he asked, struggling to hold back a yawn.

"Dead on my feet. I'm not as young as I used to be."

"Does Lindsey know you slipped out of the house last night?"

"No, but I should never have stayed out that late."

Steve didn't have any argument there. They'd left the Albertson's store when a stock boy stumbled upon them in the wine section, embarrassing Meg no end — although Steve had rather enjoyed the way her blush had brightened her cheeks.

With no other idea of where to take her at that hour, Steve had driven down to Alki Point in west Seattle, where they sat on the beach and talked.

They hadn't discussed anything of earth-shattering importance, but he discovered that they had a great deal in common. Mostly, he discovered that he liked Meg. He was already well aware of what Meg, the sensuous and beautiful woman, was capable of doing to him physically. Last night, he learned about Meg, the person.

They hadn't kissed again. Steve was convinced they both knew how dangerous kissing had become. It wouldn't take much for their kisses to lead to more . . . a *lot* more. And when that happened, he didn't plan to have it take place on a public beach.

He didn't know where the time had gone, but when he'd looked at his watch he'd been shocked. Meg, too. It was after three in the morning. They'd rushed their farewells without making arrangements to see each other again.

"When can we get together?" he asked.

"I don't know. . . ."

Was this how it was going to be? Would they have to start over each and every time they met? "Would you rather we didn't meet again?" he asked.

"No," she said immediately.

"We've got to make some decisions," he said, angry with himself for not saying anything about it on that moonlit beach. They'd discussed so many different things, from politics to movies to lifelong dreams, yet hadn't talked about their own relationship.

"I know."

"Would tonight work?" he asked. "Same time?"

She hesitated and he gritted his teeth with impatience.

"Okay." The longing in her voice reassured him.

"Fine," he said, relieved. "I'll pick you up at your house at eleven."

"I have to go now."

"Yeah. Me, too."

Steve replaced the receiver and glanced up to find Nancy standing in his office doorway, her arms folded in disapproval.

"Was that Meg?" she demanded.

"That's none of your business," Steve said sharply.

"We need to talk about her and I'm tired of you putting me off."

"I'm not discussing Meg Remington with you."

"How could you date someone like her?" Nancy asked, her face wrinkled in disgust.

"Might I remind you that you were the one who introduced us?"

"Yes, but she deceived me. Steve, be serious! Can you honestly imagine introducing her to Mom and Dad?"

"Yes," he answered calmly.

Nancy threw her arms in the air. "This is your problem. You're thinking with your you-know-what."

"Nancy!"

"It's true!"

"Stay out of my business. Understand?"

"But . . ."

"I make my own decisions," Steve said forcefully.

"And your own mistakes," Nancy muttered, walking out of the room.

"We're both crazy," Meg said, sitting next to Steve in his car. She sipped from a can of cold soda, enjoying the sweet taste of it.

"Candidates for the loony bin," he agreed.

"I wasn't sure I'd be able to get away," Meg confessed. "Brenda's spending the night with Lindsey, and those two are going to be up half the night."

"Did you tell them you were leaving the house?"

"No," she said, "but I left them a note. Just in case . . . Although I'm hoping they won't come downstairs. Oh, and this time I should remember to bring home some milk."

"I was thinking Lindsey and I should have another meeting," Steve began. "Only this time I want you to bring her to the shop. I'll show her around and explain that the whole biker, ex-con routine was a joke." He waited, then looked at Meg. "What do you think?"

"I'm afraid hell hath no fury like a teenager fooled."

"That's what I was afraid you were going to say." Steve finished his drink and placed his arm around her shoulder. "One thing's for sure. I'm through with sneaking around in the middle of the night."

Meg covered her mouth as she yawned. "I'm too old for this."

"You and me both."

Meg finished her soda, too, and leaned back against Steve, his chest supporting her back. She didn't dare close her eyes for fear she'd fall asleep.

"Nancy isn't any too happy about me seeing you, either."

"I'll talk to her, explain everything." Except that, like Lindsey, Steve's sister probably wouldn't be too pleased.

"It's settled, then," Steve said. "I'll talk to Lindsey and you'll talk to Nancy. Neither one of them is going to enjoy being the butt of a joke, but it wasn't like we planned this. Besides, it serves them right for manipulating us like they did."

"You'd think they'd be pleased," Meg inserted. "Their plan worked — not the way they wanted, mind you, but we're seeing each other and that's the whole point. Right?"

Steve chuckled and stroked her hair. "Right."

"I wish it wasn't like this," Meg whispered.

Steve kissed the top of her head. "So do I."

Meg smiled, twisting in his arms so they faced each other.

Steve's hands lingered on her face. His mouth was so close she could feel his breath against her cheek. A shiver of awareness skittered down her spine.

Meg closed her eyes and lifted her mouth to Steve's. He hesitated for a fraction of a second, as if he had second thoughts about what might happen next.

His kiss was warm and gentle. But his gentleness didn't last long. There was a hunger in Steve, a hunger in Meg that flared to life like a fire stoked.

"Meg . . ."

"I know . . . I know."

"Tomorrow," he said and drew in a deep, even breath.

"Tomorrow," she repeated, but she had no idea what she was agreeing to. She opened her eyes and leaned back. "What about tomorrow?"

"We'll talk to Lindsey and Nancy."

"Okay."

Fifteen minutes later, Steve dropped her off at the house.

It wasn't until he drove away that she realized she'd left her purse in his car. Her purse with the key to her house . . .

"Damn," she muttered, hurrying into the backyard, hoping Lindsey had forgotten to lock the sliding glass door. She hadn't; it was locked tight.

No help for it — she searched until she found the spare key, hidden under one of the flowerpots on her porch. It'd been there for so many years she wasn't sure it would work.

Luckily it did. As quietly as she could, Meg slipped into the house.

She climbed the stairs and tiptoed into her room. She undressed without turning on the light and was in bed minutes later.

The neighbor's German shepherd barked, obviously from inside their house, and Lindsey looked up from painting her toenails. "There it is again," she said.

"I heard it, too," Brenda said.

"Wolf doesn't bark without a reason."

Ever curious, Brenda walked over to the bedroom window and peered into the yard below. After a moment, she whirled around.

"There's someone in your backyard," she whispered, wide-eyed.

"This isn't the time for jokes," Lindsey said, continuing to paint her toenails a bright shade of pink. "We were discussing my mother, remember?"

Brenda didn't move away from the window. "There *is* someone there."

"Who?"

"It's a man. . . . Oh, my goodness, come and look."

The panic in her friend's voice made Lindsey catapult to a standing position. Walking on her heels to keep her freshly painted toenails off the carpet, she hobbled toward the window.

Brenda was right; she *did* see someone in the yard. "Turn the lights off," she hissed.

Lindsey's heart lodged in her throat as she recognized the dark form. "It's Steve Conlan!" She saw him clearly in the moonlight; he wasn't even making any attempt to hide.

"What's that in his hand?"

Lindsey focused her attention on the object Steve was carrying. It looked like a purse. Gasping, she twisted away from the window and placed her back against the wall. She gestured wildly toward the phone.

"What's wrong?" Brenda cried. "Are you

having an asthma attack?"

Lindsey shook her head. "He broke in to the house and stole my mother's purse." Brenda handed her the phone and Lindsey dialed 911 as fast as her nervous fingers would let her.

She barely gave the operator time to answer. "There's a man in our backyard," she whispered frantically. "He took my mother's purse."

The emergency operator seemed to have a thousand questions she wanted Lindsey to answer. Lindsey did the best she could.

"He's a convicted felon. . . . I can give you the name of his probation officer if you want. Just hurry!" she pleaded.

"Officers have been dispatched."

"Please, please hurry." Lindsey was afraid that unless the police arrived within the next minute Steve would make a clean getaway.

Steve debated whether he should leave Meg's purse on the front porch. It would be easy enough to tuck it inside the mailbox, but then she might not find it until much later the next day.

He walked around the house to the back-yard, thinking there might be someplace he could put it where she'd find it in the morning.

There wasn't.

The only thing he'd managed to do was rouse the neighbor's dog. He would've rung the doorbell and given her the silly thing if there'd been any lights on, but apparently she'd gone to bed. He wasn't especially eager to confront Lindsey, either. Not yet.

He still hadn't made up his mind, when he heard a noise from behind him.

"Police! Freeze!"

Was this a joke? Maybe not — whoever it was sounded serious. He froze.

"Put the purse down and turn around slowly."

Once more Steve did as instructed. With his arms raised, he turned to find two police officers with their weapons drawn and pointed at him.

"Looks like we caught ourselves a burglar," one of them said, switching on a huge flashlight.

"Caught him redhanded," the other agreed.

Six

"If you'd let me explain," Steve said, squinting against the light at the two officers. A dog barked ferociously in the next-door neighbor's yard. A man in pajamas had let the dog out and joined the audience.

"Do you always carry a woman's purse?"

"It belongs to —"

"My mother."

Although Steve couldn't see her face, he recognized the righteous tones as belonging to Meg's daughter. Lindsey and her friend stood beside the two officers and looked as if they'd gladly provide the rope for a hanging.

"Wolf." The neighbour silenced the German shepherd, but made no move to go inside.

"My name's Steve Conlan," Steve said, striving to come across as sane and reasonable. This was, after all, merely a misunderstanding.

"I wouldn't believe him if I were you," Lindsey advised the officers. "It might not be his real name." Then in lower tones she added, "He has a criminal record. I happen to know for a fact that he's a convicted felon."

"I'm not a felon," Steve growled. "And it *is* my real name. Officers, if you'd give me the opportunity to —"

"His parole officer's name is Earl Markham." Lindsey cut him off, her voice indignant. "He told me himself!"

"I know Earl Markham," the younger of the two policemen said. "And he is a parole officer."

"I know him, too," Steve barked impatiently. "We went to high school together."

"Yeah, right."

The scorn in Lindsey's voice reminded Steve of Meg when she was furious with him. Like mother, like daughter, it seemed.

"If you'd let me explain." Steve tried again, struggling to stay calm. It wasn't easy with two guns aimed at him and a man in pajamas clutching the collar of a huge dog — thank goodness for the fence. Not to mention a couple of teenage girls accusing him of who knew what.

"Don't listen to him," the other girl was saying. "He lies! He had us believing all kinds of things, and all because he thought we were Lindsey's mother."

A short silence followed her announcement. "Say that again?" the older officer muttered. "How well do you know this man?"

"My name's Steve Conlan." Steve tried yet again.

"Which may or may not be his real name." This, too, came from Lindsey's friend.

"If you'll let me get my wallet, I'll prove who I am," Steve assured them. He made an effort to sound vaguely amused by the whole situation. He lowered one arm and started to move his hand toward his back pocket.

"Keep your hands up where I can see them," the older cop snapped.

"What's going on?" The voice drifted down from the upstairs area of the house. A sweetly feminine, slightly groggy voice.

Steve glanced up, and to his great relief saw Meg's face framed in the second-floor window.

"Meg," Steve shouted, grateful that she'd finally heard the commotion. "Tell these men who I am, so they can put their weapons away."

"Steve?" she cried, shocked. "What are you doing at my house?"

132

"Do you know this man?" the cop asked, tilting his head back and shouting up at Meg.

"Ma'am, would you mind stepping outside?" the second officer asked. He mumbled something Steve couldn't hear under his breath.

"I'll be right down," Meg told them, and Steve watched her turn away from the window.

"Have you been sneaking around seeing my mother?"

"Lindsey, it's not like it seems," Steve said, experiencing a twinge of guilt at the way he'd misled the girl. He'd planned to talk to Meg's daughter soon, but he hadn't intended to do it in front of the police.

"I'd be more interested to find out why he has your mother's purse, if I were you," the second teenager said.

"I already know why he's got Mom's purse," Lindsey said loudly. "He stole it."

"No, I didn't!" Steve rolled his eyes. "I was trying to return it."

"You have my purse?" This was from Meg. "Oh, hello, Mr. Robinson. Hi, Wolf. I think everything's under control here." Man and dog went back inside a moment later.

"My purse!" she said again.

Steve relaxed and lowered his arms. "You

left it in my car," he said.

"Thank goodness you found it." Meg, at least, displayed the appropriate amount of appreciation. "I didn't know when I'd get it back."

Now that the flashlight wasn't blinding him and the officers had returned the guns to their holsters, Steve saw Meg for the first time. In fact, he couldn't take his eyes off her. She'd thrown a flimsy cotton robe over her baby-doll pajamas but despite that, they revealed a length of sleek, smooth thigh whenever she moved. The top was low-cut and the robe gaped open and . . . Meg grabbed the lapels and held them together with both hands. It didn't help much.

Steve was afraid he wasn't the only one who'd noticed Meg's attire. Both officers looked approvingly in her direction. Steve was about to ask the younger of the two to wipe the grin off his face, but he held his breath and counted backward from ten.

He got to five. "Lindsey, go get your mother a coat."

"I don't have to take orders from you," the girl snapped.

Meg blinked and seemed to realize that despite the robe, such as it was, her night-wear left little to the imagination.

In an apparent effort to deflect a shouting

134

match, one officer asked Lindsey a few questions, while the other engaged Steve and Meg in conversation.

"You know this man?" he asked Meg.

"Yes, of course. His name's Steve Conlan."

"Steve Conlan." The officer made note of it on a small pad. "That's what he said earlier."

Steve pulled out his wallet and flipped it open, silently thrusting it out. The cop glanced at it and nodded.

"He didn't steal my purse, either," Meg went on.

Steve cast the other man an I-told-you-so look, but said nothing.

"You went out with Steve behind my back?" Lindsey cried, peering around the second policeman. Her eyes narrowed. "I can't *believe* you'd do something like that — after our talk and everything."

Meg cast her a guilty look. "We'll discuss this later."

But Lindsey wasn't going to be so easily dissuaded. "After our talk, I really, really thought I was getting through to you. Now I see how wrong I was."

"If you'd give me a chance to explain . . ." Steve began, wanting to avoid an argument between Meg and her daughter.

Static from the police officer's walkie-talkie was followed by a muffled voice. The two men were obviously being dispatched to another location.

"Everything okay here?" the policeman asked Meg.

"It's fine."

"Young lady?"

Lindsey folded her arms and pointed her nose toward the night sky. "All I can say is that my mother's a serious disappointment to me."

"I'm afraid I can't help you there."

"I didn't think you could," she said, shaking her head. "I thought better of her than this — sneaking out at night to see a man of . . . of low moral fiber."

"Lindsey!"

"Why don't we all go inside and discuss this," Steve suggested. He felt more than a little ridiculous standing in Meg's yard, and he was eager to clear the air between Lindsey and him.

"I have nothing to say to either of you," Lindsey said. She marched into the house, with Brenda scurrying behind.

Steve watched them stomp off in single file and released a deep breath. He was about to apologize for having made such a mess of things, when Meg whirled around to face him.

"I can't believe you!"

Steve ran his fingers through his hair. Meg didn't seem to grasp that this ordeal hadn't exactly been a pleasure for him, either.

"I apologize, Meg." He did feel bad about all the trouble he'd caused, but he'd only been trying to help. When he'd found her purse, returning it had seemed the best thing to do. He didn't want her wondering where it was, and he'd honestly thought he could do it without ending up in jail.

"How dare you tell my daughter to get me a coat."

Steve's head jerked up. His throat tightened with the strength of his anger. "I nearly got myself arrested — thanks to your daughter, I might add — and *you're* upset because I objected to you traipsing around in front of the neighborhood half-naked?"

Meg opened her mouth and then closed it.

"Okay," he amended, "you are wearing a robe, although it's not much of one. Neither of those cops could take their eyes off you. I supposed you enjoyed the attention."

"Don't be ridiculous! I came downstairs as fast as I could, in order to help you."

"You call parading in front of those men like that *helping* me? All I needed was for

137

you to identify me so I could leave. That's all." His words grew louder. He was close to losing his cool and he knew it.

"I think you'd better go," Meg said, pointing in the direction of the street. Steve noticed with satisfaction that her finger shook.

"I'm out of here," he told her, "and not a minute too soon. You might have appreciated the embarrassment I endured trying to do you a favor, but I can see you don't. Which is fine by me."

"Like *you* didn't embarrass *me?*" she shouted.

"You weren't the one who had a gun pointed at you and a kid claiming you were a menace to society."

"Lindsey was only repeating what you'd told her." Meg pushed the hair away from her face, using both hands. "This isn't working."

"Wrong," he said sharply. "It's working all too well. You make me crazy, and I don't like it."

"But . . ."

"If I'm going to get arrested, I want it to be for someone who's willing to acknowledge the trouble I've gone through for her." Certain he was making no sense whatsoever, Steve stalked over to his car and drove away.

■ ■ ■ ■

Meg squared her shoulders and drew her flimsy robe more tightly around her as she opened the screen door and walked back inside. The exhaust from Steve's car lingered in the yard, reminding her how angry he'd been when he left.

She was angry, too. And confused.

It didn't help to find Lindsey and Brenda sitting in the darkened living room waiting for her.

"You should both be in bed," Meg told them.

"We want to talk to you first," Lindsey announced, her hands folded on her knees.

"Not tonight," she said shortly. "I'm tired and upset."

"You!" Lindsey cried. "Brenda and I are exhausted, but that doesn't matter. What does is that you broke your word."

"I didn't promise not to see Steve again," Meg told her. She'd been careful about that.

Meg went back to the door and stood in front of the screen, half hoping Steve would return — not knowing what she'd say or do if he did.

"You've been sneaking out of the house to see him, haven't you?"

Meg lifted one shoulder in a shrug.

"You have!" Lindsey was outraged. "When?"

Meg lifted the other shoulder.

"Can't I trust you anymore?"

"Lindsey, Steve's not exactly what he said he was."

"I'll just bet," she muttered. "He's got you fooled, hasn't he? You'd believe anything he says because that's what you *want* to believe. You're so crazy about this guy you can't even see what's right in front of your face."

If she'd been a little less upset herself, Meg might've been willing to set the record straight then and there. "We want to talk to you," Meg told her daughter. "Steve and I, together, and explain everything."

"Never!"

"Mrs. Remington, don't let him fool you," Brenda threw in dramatically.

"Let's not worry about this now," she said as defeat settled over her. "It's late and I have to be at the store early in the morning."

Lindsey stood, her hands clenched at her sides. "I want you to promise me you won't see him again."

"Lindsey, please."

"If you don't, Mom, I'll never be able to trust you again."

■ ■ ■ ■

"It's time we had a little talk," Nancy said, bringing a steaming cup of coffee to the breakfast table. After the night he'd had, the last thing Steve wanted was a tête-à-tête with his troublesome younger sister.

"No, thanks."

Nancy left the table, taking the coffee with her.

"Hey, I want the coffee."

"Oh." She brought it back and slipped into the chair across from him. "Something's bothering you."

"Nothing gets past you, does it?" He almost scalded his mouth in his eagerness to get some caffeine into his system.

"Can you tell me what's wrong?" She stared at him with big brown eyes that suggested she could solve all his problems, if only he'd let her.

"No."

"It has to do with that Meg, doesn't it?"

Steve mumbled a noncommittal reply. He didn't care to discuss Meg Remington just then. What he'd told Meg was the simple truth — she made him crazy. No woman had ever affected him as powerfully as she did. After the way they'd parted, he doubted they'd see each other again, and damn it all, that wasn't what he wanted.

"She's not the woman for you," Nancy said, her eyes solemn.

"Nancy," he said in a low voice, "don't say any more. Okay?"

She closed her eyes, shaking her head. "You're falling in love with her."

"No, I'm not," he muttered. Cradling the mug in both hands, he tried the coffee again, sipping from the edge to avoid burning his mouth.

"Thou protest too much," she told him, with a sanctimonious sigh. "I'm afraid you've made it necessary for me to take matters into my own hands. Someone's got to look out for your best interests."

Steve lowered the mug and glared at his sister. "What did you do *this* time?"

"Nothing yet. There's this woman, a widow I met on campus, and I'd like you to get to know her. She's nothing like Meg, but as far as I'm concerned . . ."

"No!" He wasn't listening to another word. The last time his sister had roped him into her schemes he'd met a crazy woman with an even crazier daughter. No more.

"But Steve . . ."

"You heard me." The chair made a scraping sound against the tile floor as he stood.

142

"I won't be home for dinner."

Nancy stood, too. "When will you be back?"

Steve regarded her suspiciously. "I don't know. Why?"

"Because the least you can do is meet Sandy."

Steve gritted his teeth. "You invited her to the house?"

"Don't worry — I didn't mention you. I wanted the two of you to meet casually. She's nervous about dating again, and I was afraid if I told her about my big, bad brother she'd run in the opposite direction."

"That's what I'm going to do. If you want to work on anyone's love life, you might try your own."

"All right, all right," Nancy said, sounding defeated. "Just stay away from Meg, okay? The woman's bad news."

Steve's laugh was humorless. "You're telling me?"

A week passed. Steve refused to dwell on his confrontation with Meg. He didn't call her and she didn't phone him, either.

He hated to end it all, but he didn't see any other option.

He missed her, though. He tried to tell himself otherwise. Tried to convince himself

143

a man has his pride. Tried not to think about her.

And failed.

Early one afternoon, Nancy came by the shop with a friend. They were on their way to a movie, or so Nancy claimed.

Nancy smiled a little-sister smile and cheerfully asked Steve if he'd give Sandy an estimate on repairing her fender.

Sandy was petite. Cute. A little fragile.

It didn't take Steve long to figure out that this Sandy was the same one Nancy had wanted him to meet. The widow. The woman who'd save him from Meg's clutches.

"Pleased to meet you," Steve said, wiping his greasy hands on the pink cloth he had tucked in his hip pocket.

Nancy smiled innocently, looking pleased with herself.

"I'll have a written estimate for you by the time you two get back here."

"You don't have to work late again, do you?" Nancy asked, not even attempting to be coy.

Steve could already see what was coming. His conniving sister was about to wrangle a dinner invitation out of him. One that meant he'd be stuck entertaining Sandy.

"I'm afraid I'm tied up this evening," he

said stiffly.

"Oh, darn. I was hoping you could take Sandy and me to dinner."

"Sorry," he said. "Now, if you'll excuse me . . ."

"It was a pleasure to meet you, Mr. Conlan."

"The pleasure was mine," he said and turned away.

Unfortunately, it didn't end with Sandy. His sister had several other friends with dented fenders or cracked windshields. They all seemed to need estimates in the days that followed.

"The next time a woman comes in and asks for me, I'm unavailable," he told his crew. Steve made sure that on her next visit Nancy would know he didn't have time for her matchmaking games. He told her as much when she stopped by — alone — a couple of days later.

"I was only trying to help."

"Thanks, but no thanks." He sat at his desk, making his way through the piles of paperwork stacked in front of him.

Nancy expelled a sigh. "You aren't seeing Meg again, are you?"

His hand tightened around the pen. "That's none of your business."

"Yes, it is! A woman like that could ruin

145

your life."

In some ways she already had, but Nancy wouldn't understand. Whenever he met another woman, Steve found himself comparing her to Meg. Invariably everyone else fell short. Far short. He was miserable without her.

Nancy left, and Steve leaned back in his chair, studying the phone. All it would take was one call. He wouldn't have to mention the incident with the police. He could even make a joke of it, maybe buy her a pair of flannel pajamas. The kind that went from her neck to her feet. They'd both laugh, say how sorry they were and put an end to this stalemate.

Then he'd take her in his arms, hold her and kiss her. This was the part he dwelled on most. The reconciliation.

"Steve." Gary Wilcox stuck his head in the office door.

Steve jerked his attention away from the phone.

"There's someone here to see you. A woman."

Impatience made Steve's blood boil. "What did I say earlier? I gave specific instructions to tell any of my sister's friends that I'm unavailable."

"But —"

"Is that so hard to understand?"

"Nope," Gary said without emotion. "I don't have a problem doing that, if it's what you really want, but I kinda had the feeling this one's special."

Knowing his foreman had cast an appreciative eye at the widow, Steve suspected it was Sandy who'd dropped by unannounced. "You talk to her."

"Me?"

"Yeah, you."

"What am I supposed to say?"

Steve rubbed a hand down his tired face. Did he have to do everything himself? "I don't know, just say whatever seems appropriate. I promise you Nancy won't be sending any more eligible women to the shop."

"Nancy didn't send this one."

The pen slipped from Steve's hands and rolled across the desk. "Who did?"

"She didn't say. All I got was her name. Meg Remington. I seem to recall hearing it mentioned a time or two — generally when you were upset."

Steve pushed back his chair and slowly stood. His heart reacted with a swift, furious pace. "Meg's here?"

"That's what I've been trying to tell you for the last five minutes."

Steve sank back into the chair. "Send her in."

A mischievous grin danced across Gary's mouth. "That's what I thought you'd say."

Steve stood, then sat back down and busied himself with things on his desk. He wanted Meg to think he was busy. The minute she walked into the room, he'd set everything aside.

A full five minutes passed and still she didn't show up. Steve came out of his office and ran into Gary, who frowned and shook his head. "She's gone."

"Gone?"

Gary nodded. "The only thing I can figure out is that she must've overheard you say you weren't available and left."

Steve muttered a four-letter word and hurried out. He wasn't sure where he'd find her, but he wasn't going to let her walk out of his life.

She wasn't at the bookstore and he didn't see her car at home. He tried the grocery store, too, for good measure. Without success.

It wasn't until nearly seven that he drove to her house again. That he was willing to confront her daughter was a sign of how desperate he'd become.

He stood on her front porch and rang the

doorbell. Waiting for someone to answer, he buried his hands deep in his pockets. A preventive action, he realized, to keep from reaching for her the instant she appeared.

"Just a minute," he heard her call.

Then the door opened and Meg was standing there.

His gaze drifted over her. He'd planned to play it cool, casually mention that he was in the neighborhood and heard she'd stopped by the office. Their eyes met, held, and Steve forgot about hiding his feelings. She wore a pretty pale blue summer dress.

"Hello, Steve."

"Hello."

The screen door stood between them.

They continued to stare at each other.

"Can I come in?" he asked. Pride be damned. It'd been cold comfort in the past two weeks. If he had to apologize, or grovel or beg forgiveness, then so be it. He wanted her back in his life.

"Of course." She unlatched the door and pushed it open.

Steve stepped inside. He could barely breathe, never mind think. Pulling her into his arms didn't seem appropriate, but that was all he wanted to do.

"Where's Lindsey?" he managed to ask.

Meg's voice was breathy and uneven.

"She's out for the evening."

He needed to touch her. Reaching up, he cupped her cheek in his rough palm. Slowly, Meg closed her eyes and leaned her head into his hand.

"I had to come here," he whispered.

"I'm so sorry. About everything."

"Me, too."

Unable to wait a second longer, Steve folded her in his arms and brought her mouth to his. Gentleness was beyond him, his hunger as great as any he'd ever known.

Meg grabbed his shirt as if she needed an anchor, something to secure her during the wild, sensual storm. He backed her against the door.

Meg gasped, and Steve moved a few inches away. With his hands framing her cheeks, he studied her beautiful face. Her shoulders were heaving, and he realized his own breathing was just as labored.

He rubbed the pad of his thumb across her moist, swollen lips. The action was unhurried — an apology for his roughness, his eagerness.

She moaned softly and he kissed her again. Gently. With restraint. Her arms were around his neck, and Steve had never tasted a sweeter kiss.

"I was going to call," he told her, burying

his face in the slope of her neck. "A thousand times I told myself I'd call. Every minute apart from you was torture."

"I wanted to call you, too."

"I'm glad. . . ."

"You were right," Meg confessed. "I should've been wearing something more . . . discreet."

"I was jealous, pure and simple." He felt her smile against the side of his face and smiled, too.

"I would've been jealous if the situation had been reversed."

"Don't worry. I didn't date a single one of the women Nancy arranged for me to meet."

Meg jerked back. "What women?"

"Ah . . . it's not important."

"It is to me."

He knew it would've been to him, as well, so he explained. "Nancy felt it was necessary to save me from a loose woman, so she introduced me to some of her friends."

"And you refused to go out with them." Meg sounded pleased.

"All I want to do is talk to Lindsey. Get things straightened out."

"Me, too. But we can't right now."

"So I see."

"Hold me," she said, nestling in his arms.

"I don't want you to leave for a long, long time."

Steve planted tiny kisses along the side of her neck, marking his way back to her lips. "When will Lindsey be back?" he whispered.

"She's spending the night at Brenda's."

His hold tightened. "Meg," he said, then kissed her with a hunger he couldn't deny. "I want to make love to you. There's a lot we have to discuss before we make that kind of commitment, but we have an opportunity to do that now, don't we?"

"Mmm."

He kissed her again, pacing himself. "Thank God you dropped in at the office. I don't know how long it would've taken me to come to my senses otherwise."

"The office?" Meg repeated, breaking away from him. "I was never at your office."

SEVEN

"It doesn't matter if you were at my office or not," Steve said, kissing Meg again. Slowly. Thoroughly.

She couldn't manage even a token resistance, although her mind whirled with questions.

She was starved for the taste of him. Starved for his touch. Starved for *him.* The loneliness had been suffocating. Before she'd met Steve, her life had seemed just fine. Then within a matter of weeks she'd realized how empty everything was without him.

"I've missed you so much," she told him between deep kisses.

"Me, too."

"You should've phoned," she whispered.

"You, too."

"I know."

"I'm crazy about you."

She was so tempted to throw caution to

the wind and make love with this man who excited her so much. Who made her feel alive.

If ever the moment was right it was now, with Lindsey gone until morning.

But . . .

The questions returned. There'd only been one man in her life, her ex-husband, Lindsey's father, and by the time they'd divorced Meg had felt like a failure as a wife. Inadequate. Unresponsive.

"Steve . . . Steve." Her fingers were in Steve's hair as his mouth roamed over her throat. "Stop, please."

He went still, his lips pressed against the hollow of her throat. "You want me to stop? Now?"

"Please . . . for just a minute. Did you say you thought I'd been to your office?" She wanted that confusion cleared up first.

"It's what Gary told me." He raised his head, eyes clouded with passion. "It doesn't matter — I'm here now. I've missed you so much. I can't believe either of us let this go on so long."

"But it does matter," she argued. "Because I wasn't there."

Steve shut his eyes and seemed to be fighting something in himself. Finally, he straightened and eased away from her.

154

"I'm glad you're here," she whispered. "I've missed you, too. It's just that before we . . ." She felt as though her face was on fire. How she wished she was more experienced, more sophisticated. "You know."

"Make love," he finished for her.

"Yes . . . We should come to some sort of understanding. It's like you said — we should talk first."

Steve took her by the hand. He led her into the living room and chose the big overstuffed chair that was her favorite.

He sat and, reaching up, pulled her onto his lap. "So let's talk."

"Okay," she said, hating the way her voice trembled.

"First I want to clear something up. You say you *didn't* stop by my office this afternoon?"

"No. I was at the store until after six."

"I didn't see you there."

"I was in the back room, processing orders." Because she was afraid he'd think she was lying in order to save face, she added, "You can check with Laura if you want."

Steve frowned. "I believe you. Why wouldn't I?" He studied her. "But that isn't why you stopped us just now, is it?"

155

Meg lowered her gaze. "No," she whispered.

"I didn't think so. Are you going to tell me?"

"Tell you what?" Steve's arm went around her waist. It felt good to be this close to him.

"I suspect your reluctance has to do with your marriage."

"My marriage?"

"It doesn't take a detective to figure out that your ex-husband hurt you badly."

"No divorce is easy," Meg admitted, "but I'm not an emotional cripple, if that's what you mean."

"It isn't." He drew her even closer and kissed her again. She kissed him back, offering him her heart, her soul, her body . . .

"I can't seem to keep my hands off you," he murmured. "I wanted to talk to you about your marriage. Instead, I'm a second away from ravishing you."

And she was a second away from letting him.

"It was a friendly divorce," Meg insisted, returning to the subject he'd introduced. It wasn't a comfortable one — but it was safer than touching and kissing and where that would lead.

Steve eyed her suspiciously. "How

friendly?" he asked.

"We parted amicably. It was a mutual decision."

"What caused the divorce?"

Meg closed her eyes and sighed. "He had a girlfriend," she said, trying not to reveal her bitterness. For years she'd kept the feelings of hurt and betrayal buried deep.

In the beginning, that had been for Lindsey's sake. Later, she was afraid to face the anger for fear of what it would do to her. "Dave didn't love me anymore," she said, in an unemotional voice. As if it didn't matter. As if it had never mattered.

"What about Lindsey? He abandoned her, too?"

"He knew I'd always be there for her, and I will. He lives in California now."

"What about his commitment to you and his daughter? That wasn't important to him?"

"I don't know — you'd need to ask Dave about that."

"How long did this business with the girlfriend go on before he told you about her?"

"I don't know," she said again. She had her suspicions, plenty of them, but none she was willing to discuss with Steve. "I do know that when Dave got around to telling me he wanted a divorce, she was pregnant."

"In other words, you felt there was nothing you could do but step aside?"

"I had no problem doing that." Maybe if she'd loved Dave more, she would've been willing to fight for him. But by the time Dave told her about Brittany, she wanted out of the marriage. Just plain out.

"So you got divorced."

"Yes, with no fuss at all. He gave me what I wanted."

"And what was that?"

"He was willing to let me raise Lindsey." She shook her head. "It's not what you're thinking."

"And what am I thinking?"

She placed the back of her hand against her forehead and gave him a forlorn look, like the heroine of a silent movie. "That the divorce traumatized me."

"I wasn't thinking that at all," he assured her. "Your marriage had already taken care of that."

Meg dropped her hand, then raised it again to brush away her tears. How well Steve understood.

"It wasn't enough that your husband had an affair. When he walked out on you and Lindsey, he made sure you blamed yourself for his infidelity, didn't he?" She didn't respond, and he asked her a second time, his voice gentle. "Didn't he?"

Meg jerked her head away for fear he'd read the truth in her eyes. "It's over now. . . . It was all a long time ago."

"But it isn't over. If it was, we'd be upstairs making love instead of sitting here talking. You haven't been able to trust another man since Dave."

"No," she whispered, her head lowered.

"Oh, baby," he said tenderly, gathering her in his arms. "I'm so sorry."

She blinked rapidly in an effort to forestall more tears. "I trust you," she told him, and she knew instinctively that Steve would never betray his wife or walk away from his family.

"You do trust me," he said, "otherwise you wouldn't have let me get this close to you. Just be warned. I intend to get a whole lot closer, and soon."

With anyone else Meg would have felt threatened, but with Steve it felt like a promise. A promise she wanted him to fulfill.

"It's better that we wait to make love," he surprised her by adding.

"It is?" Her head shot up.

"I want to clear the air with Lindsey first," he told her. "Get things settled between us.

I'd much rather be her friend than her foe."

"And I'd like to be Nancy's friend, too," Meg said.

He smiled. "Those girls don't know what they started — or where it's going to end."

"Exactly where are we going?" Lindsey asked, staring out the car window.

"I already told you." Meg was losing patience with her daughter.

"To see Steve at work?"

"Yes."

"Work release, you mean."

"Lindsey!" Meg said emphatically. She'd never known her to be this difficult. "Steve has his own business. We both thought if you could see him at work, you'd know that what he told you about being an ex-con was all a farce."

Lindsey remained sullen for several minutes, then asked, "Why'd he say all those things if they weren't true?"

Her daughter had a valid point, but they'd gone over this same ground a dozen times. "We wanted you to dislike him."

Unfortunately Steve's plan had worked all too well. And Meg had obviously done an equally good job with Nancy, because his sister didn't want him continuing to see her, either. What a mess they'd created.

"Why wouldn't you and Steve want me to like him?" Lindsey asked.

"I've already explained, and I don't feel like repeating the story yet again," Meg said. "Suffice it to say I'm not especially proud of our behavior."

Lindsey pouted, but didn't ask any more questions.

Meg pulled into the parking lot at Steve's business and watched as Lindsey took in everything — the well-established body shop, the customers, the neat surroundings.

There were three large bays all filled with vehicles in various states of disrepair. Men dressed in blue-striped coveralls worked on the cars.

"They *all* look like they came straight from a prison yard," Lindsey mumbled under her breath.

"Lindsey," Meg pleaded, wanting this meeting to go well. "At least give Steve a chance."

"I did once, and according to you he lied."

Once more, Meg had no argument. "Just listen to him, okay?"

"All right, but I'm not making any promises."

The shop smelled of paint and grease; the scents weren't unpleasant. There was a small waiting area with a coffeepot, paper

161

cups and several outdated magazines.

"Hello," Meg said to the man standing behind the counter. "I'm Meg Remington. Steve is expecting me."

The man studied her. "*You're* Meg Remington?" he asked.

"Yes."

"You don't look like the Meg Remington who was in here last week."

"I beg your pardon?"

"Never mind, Gary," Steve said, walking out from the office. He smiled warmly when he saw Meg. Lindsey sat in the waiting area, reading a two-year-old issue of *Car and Driver* as if it contained the answers to life's questions.

"Hello, Lindsey," Steve said.

"Hello," she returned in starched tones.

"Would you and your mother care to come into my office?"

"Will we be safe?"

A hint of a smile cracked Steve's mouth, but otherwise he didn't let on that her question had amused him. "I don't think there'll be a problem."

"All right, fine, since you insist." She set aside the magazine and stood.

Steve ushered them into the spotlessly clean office and gestured at the two chairs on the other side of his desk. "Please, have a seat."

They did, with Lindsey perched stiffly on the edge of hers.

"Would you like something to drink?" he asked.

"No, thanks."

Meg didn't think she'd ever seen Lindsey less friendly. It wasn't like her to behave like this. Presumably she thought she was protecting her mother.

"I have a confession to make," Steve said, after an awkward moment. He leaned back in his chair.

"Shouldn't you be telling this to the police?" Lindsey asked.

"Not this time." His eyes connected with Meg's. She tried to tell him how sorry she was, but nothing she'd said had changed Lindsey's attitude.

"I did something I regret," Steve continued undaunted. "I lied to you. And as often happens when people lie, it came back to haunt me."

"I'm afraid I was a party to this falsehood myself," Meg added.

"How do you know it's really a lie?" Lindsey demanded of Meg. "Steve could actually be a convicted criminal. He might be sitting behind that desk, but how do we

163

know if what he says is true?"

Meg rolled her eyes.

"Who are you *really,* Steve Conlan?" Lindsey leaned forward, planting both hands on the edge of his desk.

"I'm exactly who I appear to be. I'm thirty-eight years old. Unmarried. I own this shop and have ten full-time employees."

"Can you prove it?"

"Of course."

A knock sounded on the door.

"Come in," Steve called.

The man who'd greeted her when she first arrived stuck his head inside the door. He smiled apologetically. "Sorry to interrupt, but Sandy Janick's on the phone."

Steve frowned. "Are we working on Sandy's vehicle?" he wanted to know. "I don't remember seeing a work order."

"No, she's that friend your sister was trying to set you up with. Remember?"

"Tell her I'll call her back," Steve said without hesitating.

Meg bristled. He'd admitted that his sister had been playing matchmaker. So Nancy had set him up with another woman. Probably one without a troublesome teenager and a bunch of emotional garbage she was dragging around from a previous marriage. Meg tried to swallow the lump forming in

164

her throat.

"Gary," Steve said, stopping the other man from leaving. "Would you kindly tell Lindsey who owns this shop?"

"Sure," the other man said with a grin. "Mostly the IRS."

"I'm serious," Steve said impatiently.

Gary chuckled. "Last I heard it was Walter Milton at Key Bank. Oops, there goes the phone again." He was gone an instant later.

"Walter Milton," Lindsey said skeptically. "So you really *don't* own this business."

"Walter Milton's my banker and a good friend."

"So is Earl Markham, your parole officer," Lindsey snapped. "A high school friend, correct?" She shook her head. "I'm afraid I can't believe you, Mr. Conlan. If you were trying to get me to change my mind about you seeing my mother, it didn't work." Then turning to Meg, she said, "I wouldn't trust him if I were you. He's got a look about him. . . ."

"What look?" Meg and Steve asked simultaneously.

"You know — a criminal look. I'm sure I've seen his face before, and my guess is that it was in some post office."

Meg ground her teeth with frustration.

"Lindsey, would you please stop being so difficult?"

"I don't think it's a good idea for you to date a man who lies."

"You're right," Steve surprised them both by saying. "I should never have made up that ridiculous story about being a felon. I've learned my lesson and I won't pull that stunt again. All I'm asking is that you give me a second chance to prove myself."

"I don't think so."

Meg resisted throwing her arms in the air.

"You know what really bothers me?" Lindsey went on. "That you'd involve my mother in this stupid scam of yours. That's really low."

"I don't blame you for being angry with me," Steve said, before Meg could respond. "But don't be upset with your mother — it was my idea, not hers."

"My mother wouldn't stoop to anything that underhanded on her own."

Meg's eyes met Steve's and she wanted to weep with frustration.

"I was hoping you'd find it in your heart to forgive me," Steve said contritely, returning his attention to Lindsey. "I'd like us to be friends."

"Even if we were, that doesn't mean I approve of you seeing my mother."

"Lindsey," Meg began. "I —"

"Mom, we can't trust this guy," Lindsey interrupted. "We know how willing he is to lie. And what about that phone call just now?" She pointed at Steve. "Another woman calls and he can hardly wait to get back to her. You saw the expression on his face."

"Don't be ridiculous," Steve snapped. "I'm crazy about your mother. I wouldn't hurt her for the world."

"Yeah, whatever. That's what they all say." Lindsey had perfected the world-weary tone so beloved of teenagers everywhere.

"I've had enough, Lindsey," Meg said sternly. "I think you'd better go wait in the car."

Lindsey leapt eagerly out of her chair and rushed from the office, leaving Steve and Meg alone.

"I'm sorry," she whispered, standing.

"I'll try to talk to her again." Steve walked around the desk and pulled her into his arms. "All she needs is a little time. Eventually she'll learn to trust me." He raised her hand to his mouth and kissed the knuckles. "But one thing's for sure. . . ."

"What's that?"

"I'm through with sneaking around meeting you. I'm taking you to dinner tonight

167

and I'm coming to the front door. Lindsey will just have to accept that we're dating. In fact, I'll ask her if she'd like to join us."

"She won't," Meg said with certainty.

"I'm still going to ask. She may not like me now, but in time I'll win her heart, just the way I intend to win her mother's."

What Steve didn't seem to understand was that he'd already won hers.

At seven that night, Meg was humming softly to herself and dabbing perfume on her wrists. Steve was due any minute.

The telephone rang, but Meg didn't bother to answer. There was no point. The call was almost guaranteed to be for Lindsey. She heard the girl racing at breakneck speed for the phone, as if reaching it before the second ring was some kind of personal goal.

"Mom!" Lindsey screeched from the kitchen downstairs, reaching her in the master bath.

"I'll be right there," she called back, checking her reflection in the bathroom mirror one last time.

Lindsey yelled something else that Meg couldn't hear.

"Who is it?" Meg asked, coming out of her bedroom and hurrying downstairs.

"I already told you it's Steve," Lindsey said indifferently as she passed her leaving the kitchen.

Meg glanced at her watch and reached for the phone. "Hello."

"Hi," he said, sounding discouraged. "I ran into a problem and it looks like I'm going to be late."

"What kind of problem?" It was already later than her normal dinnertime, and Meg was hungry.

"I'm not sure yet. Sandy Janick phoned and apparently she's got a flat tire. . . ."

"Listen," Meg said with feigned cheerfulness, "why don't we cancel dinner for this evening? It sounds like you've got your hands full."

"Yes, but . . ."

"I'm hungry right now. It's no big deal — we'll have dinner another night."

Steve hesitated. "You're sure?"

"Positive." She was trembling so badly it was difficult to remain standing. Steve and Sandy. She suspected Nancy had arranged the flat tire, but if Steve couldn't see through that, then it was obvious he didn't want to. "It's not a problem," Meg insisted.

"I'll give you a call tomorrow."

"Sure. . . . That would be great." She barely heard the rest of the conversation.

He kept talking and Meg hoped she made the appropriate responses. She must have, because a couple of minutes later he hung up.

Closing her eyes, Meg exhaled and replaced the receiver.

"Mom?"

Meg turned to face her daughter.

"Is everything okay?"

She nodded, unable to chase away the burning pain that attacked the pit of her stomach and radiated out.

"Then how come you're so pale?"

"I'm fine, honey. Steve and I won't be going out to dinner after all." She tried to sound as if nothing was amiss, but her entire world seemed to be collapsing around her. "Why don't we get a pizza? Do you want to call? Order whatever you want. Okay?"

She was overreacting and knew it. If Steve was doing something underhanded, he wouldn't tell her he was meeting Sandy Janick. He'd do the same things Dave had done. He'd lie and cheat.

"I'm going to change my clothes," Meg said, heading blindly for the stairs.

She half expected Lindsey to follow her and announce that she'd been right all along, that Steve wasn't to be trusted. But

170

to Meg's astonishment, her daughter said nothing.

"I knew if anyone could help Sandy with her flat tire it would be you," Nancy said, smiling benevolently at her older brother.

Steve glanced at his watch, frustrated and angry with his sister — and himself. She'd done it again. She'd manipulated him into doing something he didn't want to do. Instead of spending the evening with Meg, he'd been trapped into helping these two out of a fix.

Leave it to his sister. Not only had Nancy and Sandy managed to get a flat, but they'd been on the Mercer Island floating bridge in the middle of rush-hour traffic. Steve had to arrange for a tow truck and then meet them at his shop. From there, they'd all ended up back at the house, and Sandy had made it clear that she was looking for a little male companionship. There was a time Steve would've jumped at the chance to console the attractive widow. But no longer.

"I can't tell you how much I appreciate your help," Sandy told him now. "Thank you so much."

"You're welcome." He looked pointedly at his watch. It was just after nine, still early enough to steal away and visit Meg. Lindsey would disapprove, but that couldn't be avoided.

The girl was proving to be more of a problem than Steve had expected. She was downright stubborn and unwilling to give him the slightest bit of credit. Well, she was dealing with a pro, and Steve wasn't about to give up on either of the Remington women. Not without a fight.

"You're leaving?" Nancy asked as Steve marched to the front door.

"Yes," he said. "Is that a problem?"

"I guess not." His sister wore a downtrodden look, as if he'd disappointed her.

"I have to be going, too," Sandy Janick said. "Again, thank you."

Steve walked her to the door and said a polite goodbye, hoping it really *was* goodbye. He wished her well, but wasn't interested in becoming her knight in shining armor. Not when there was another damsel whose interest he coveted.

He closed the door as he went to retrieve his car keys from the hall table and grab his jacket.

Nancy got up and followed him as he prepared to leave. "Where are you going?" she asked.

Steve glared at his sister. "What makes you think it's any of your business?"

"Because I have a feeling that you're off to see that . . . that floozy."

"*Floozy?* What on earth have you been reading?" Shaking his head, he muttered, "Meg isn't a floozy or a woman of ill repute or a hussy or any other silly term you want to call her. She's a single mother and a businesswoman. She owns a bookstore. She —"

"That's not what she told me."

"Listen. I'm thirty-eight years old and I won't have my little sister running my love life. Now, I helped you and your friend, but I had to break a dinner date with Meg to do it."

"Then I'm glad Sandy got that flat tire," she said defiantly.

Steve had had enough. "Stay out of my life, Nancy. I'm warning you."

His sister raised her head dramatically, as if she'd come to some momentous decision. "I'm afraid I can't do that. I'm really sorry, Steve."

"What do you mean, you *can't?*"

"I can't stand idly by and watch the brother I've always loved and admired make a complete fool of himself. Especially over a woman like *that.*"

Steve's patience was gone. Vanished. But before he could say a word, Nancy threw herself in front of him.

"I won't let you do this!" she said, stretching her arms across the door.

The phone rang just then, and Steve knew he'd been saved by the bell. Nancy flew across the room to answer it.

Hoping to make a clean getaway, Steve opened the door and dashed outside. As he'd suspected, Nancy tore out after him.

"It's for you," she called from the front porch.

Steve was already in his car and he wasn't going to be waylaid by his sister a second time.

"Tell whoever it is I'll call back."

"It's a woman."

"What's her name?"

"Lindsey," she called at the top of her voice. "And she wants to talk to you."

EIGHT

The last person Steve expected to hear from was Meg's standoffish teenage daughter. He climbed out of his car and ran up the porch steps. He walked directly past his sister and without saying a word went straight to the phone.

"Lindsey? What's the problem?" he asked. He was in no mood for games and he wanted her to know it.

"Are you alone?" Lindsey asked him.

Steve noticed that her voice was lower than usual. He assumed that meant Meg wasn't aware of her daughter's call.

"My sister's here," he answered. Nancy stood with her arms folded, frowning at him with unconcealed disapproval.

"Anyone else?" Lindsey asked, then added snidely, "Especially someone named Sandy."

It sounded as if Lindsey was jealous on her mother's behalf, which was ridiculous. The kid would be glad of an excuse to get rid of him. "No. Sandy left a few minutes ago."

"So you *were* with her," she accused.

In light of the confrontation he'd just had with his sister, Steve's hold on his patience was already strained. "Is there a reason for your call?" he asked bluntly.

"Of course," Lindsey muttered with an undignified huff. "I want to know what you said that upset my mother."

"What I said?" Steve didn't understand.

"After you called, she told me to order pizza for dinner and then she said I could have anything on it I wanted. She knows I like anchovies and she can't stand 'em. Then," Lindsey said, after a short pause, "the pizza came and she looked at me like she didn't have a clue where it came from. Something's wrong and I want you to tell me what it is."

"I have no idea."

"Mom's just not herself." Another pause, a longer one this time. "You'd better come over and talk to her."

An invitation from the veritable dragon of a daughter herself? This was a stroke of luck. "You sure you can trust me?" he couldn't resist asking.

"Not really," she said with feeling. "But I don't think I have a choice. My mom likes you although I can't figure out why."

The kid was a definite hazard to his ego, but Steve decided to let the comment pass.

"You think your mother's upset because I broke our dinner date?" he asked. "Well, I've got news for you — she's the one who called it off. She said it was no big deal."

"And you believed her?"

"Shouldn't I?"

Steve could picture the girl rolling her eyes. "Either you aren't as smart as you look, or you've been in prison for so long you don't know anything about women."

Steve didn't find either possibility flattering. "All I did was phone to tell her I was going to be late. What's so awful about that?"

"You were late because you were meeting another woman!"

"Wrong," Steve protested. "I was *helping* another woman. Actually two women, one of whom was my sister."

"Don't you get it? My dad left my mother because of another woman. He made up all these lies about where he was and what he was doing so he could be with her."

"And you're worried that your mother assumes I'm doing the same thing? Lindsey, isn't that a bit of a stretch?"

"Yes . . . no. I don't know," she said. "All

177

I know is you canceled —"

"*She* canceled."

"Your dinner date because you were meeting another woman —"

"Helping another woman and my sister."

"Whatever. All I know is that Mom hasn't been the same since, and if you care about her the way you keep saying . . ."

"I do."

"Then I suggest you get over here, and fast." The line was abruptly disconnected.

Steve stared at the receiver, then replaced it, shaking his head as he did.

"What's wrong with Meg?" Nancy asked.

Steve shrugged. "Darned if I know. No one ever told me falling in love was so complicated." Having said that, he marched out the door.

Nancy ran after him. "You're in love with her?"

"I sure am."

A huge smile lit up his sister's face. Steve stood next to his car, wondering if he was seeing things. A smile was the last reaction he would've expected from Nancy.

He muttered to himself on the short drive to Meg's house. He didn't stop muttering — about women and daughters and sisters — until he rang the doorbell.

The door was opened two seconds later

178

by Lindsey. "It took you long enough," she said.

"Lindsey, who is it?" Meg asked, stepping out from the kitchen. She'd apparently been putting away dishes, because she had a plate and a coffee mug in her hand. "Steve," she whispered, "what are you doing here?"

"Have you had dinner yet?"

"Not really," Lindsey answered for her mother. "She nibbled on a slice of pizza, but that was only so I wouldn't bug her. I ordered her favorite kind, too." She paused and grimaced. "Vegetarian. Even though *I* like anchovies and pepperoni."

"Weren't you hungry?" Steve asked, silencing Lindsey with a look.

Meg raised one shoulder in a shrug. "Not really. What about you? Did you get anything to eat?"

"Nope."

"There's leftover pizza if you're interested."

"I'm interested," he said, moving toward her. Lindsey was right — Meg seemed upset.

"You're not going to *eat,* are you?" Lindsey demanded.

"Why not?" Steve asked.

The girl sighed loudly. "What my mother needs here is reassurance. If you had a

179

romantic thought in that empty space between your ears, you'd take her in your arms and . . . and kiss her."

All Steve could do was stand there and stare. This was the same annoying girl who'd been a source of constant irritation from the moment they'd met. Something had changed, and he didn't know what or why.

"Lindsey?" Meg obviously had the same questions as Steve.

"What?" Lindsey asked. "Oh, you want to know why I changed my mind. Well, I've been thinking. If Steve really meant what he said about being friends, then I guess I'm willing to meet him halfway." This was said as if it had come at great personal sacrifice. She turned to Steve. "Actually, I can't see any way around it. It's clear to me that my mother's fallen in love with you."

"Lindsey!"

Steve enjoyed the way Meg's blush colored her pale cheeks.

"And it's equally clear to me that Steve feels the same, especially if he was willing to put up with all my insults. Frankly, I can't see fighting it any longer. What's the point? And really, I can't keep a constant eye on you two. I do have my own life."

Lindsey's change of heart was welcome

news to Steve. The kid held the all-important key to Meg's heart. He'd never win her love, if he didn't gain Lindsey's approval first.

"Don't get the idea I *like* any of this," Lindsey added — to salvage her pride, he guessed. "But I can learn to live with it."

"Great," Steve said, offering her his hand. "Let's shake on it."

Lindsey studied his hand as if she wasn't sure she wanted to touch him. But once she did, her shake was firm and confident.

"You're nothing like you were supposed to be," she muttered under her breath.

"I apologize for being such a disappointment," he said out of the corner of his mouth.

"Can't do anything about that now. Mom's crazy about you."

"I think she's pretty terrific, too."

Lindsey sighed. "So I noticed."

"What are you two talking about?" Meg asked.

"Nothing," Lindsey answered with exaggerated innocence. She looked at Steve and winked.

He returned her wink, pleased to be on solid ground with the girl. "Did someone say something about pizza?"

"I did," Meg told him. "Come into the

kitchen and I'll microwave the leftovers."

"Mother," Lindsey groaned. "I thought I could count on you to be a little more romantic. Or do I have to do everything myself?"

"What did I do wrong now?"

"Couldn't you make Steve something special?"

Meg took a moment to think this over. "I've got chicken I could make into a salad. If he doesn't like that, there's always peanut-butter-and-jelly sandwiches."

"I'd rather have the pizza," Steve interjected. He didn't want Meg wasting her time preparing a meal, all in the name of some romantic fantasy. He wanted her to talk — and to listen.

Before Lindsey could protest, Steve followed Meg into the kitchen. "Do you know what that was about?"

Meg smiled and opened the refrigerator. "Nope." She took out the pizza box and set it on the counter.

Steve climbed onto the stool. "So what happened earlier?" he asked.

Meg hesitated, separating a piece of the pizza. "I suppose Lindsey called you?"

"Yes, but I was already on my way over here."

He saw that she avoided his eyes, as she

made busywork of setting two huge slices of pizza on a plate and heating them in the microwave. "After your phone call, I had kind of a panic attack."

"About?" he prompted.

"You . . . Us."

"And?"

"And I worked it out myself. I felt pretty foolish afterward. I realized you aren't the same kind of man Dave was . . . is. If you call to say you're helping another woman, then that's exactly what you're doing."

"You thought I was seeing someone else?" Lindsey had implied as much, but he hadn't taken it seriously.

"I feel silly now," she said, setting the sizzling pizza slices in front of him. She propped her elbows on the counter and rested her chin in her palms. "It was as if the craziness of my marriage was back. You see, at one time I tried to believe Dave. He'd make up the most outrageous stories to account for the huge periods of time he was away from home, and like a naive idiot, I'd believe him." She paused. "I guess because I wanted to. But Dave's not my problem anymore."

"A leopard doesn't change his spots," Steve said, finishing off the first slice. "If Dave cheated on you, he'll cheat on his present wife, too. It stands to reason."

"I know. From what Lindsey said after her last visit to California, Dave's marriage is on shaky ground. I'm sorry for him and for his wife."

Steve offered Meg the second slice, which she declined. He'd just taken a bite when the low strains of soulful violin music drifted toward them. Steve glanced at Meg and she shrugged, perplexed.

Lindsey appeared in the kitchen, looking thoroughly disgusted. "You two need my help, don't you?"

"Help?" Steve repeated. "With what?"

"Romance." She walked into the room and took Steve's hand and then her mother's. She led them both into the living room. The furniture had been pushed to one side and the lights turned down low. Two crystal glasses and a bottle of red wine sat on the coffee table, ready to be put to good use.

"Now, I'll disappear into my room for a while," she said, "and you two can do all the things I've read about in novels."

Steve and Meg stared blankly at each other.

"Don't tell me you need help with that, too!"

"We can take it from here," Steve was quick to assure her.

"I should hope so," Lindsey muttered. With an air of superiority she headed up the stairs.

The music was sultry. Inviting. Once Lindsey was out of sight, Steve held his arms open to Meg. "Shall we dance?"

Steve could've sworn she blushed, very prettily, too, before she slipped into his embrace. He brought her close and sighed, reveling in the feel of her.

"I'm not very good at dancing," she murmured.

"Hey, don't worry. All we have to do is shift our feet a little." He laid his cheek next to hers.

He'd never had the time or the patience for romance. Or so he'd believed. Then he'd met Meg and his organized, safe, secure world had been turned upside down. Nothing had been the same since, and Steve suspected it never would be again.

Even Gary Wilcox seemed to recognize the difference between Steve's attitude toward Meg and his attitude to the other women he'd dated over the years. Steve didn't know how his foreman had figured it out, but he had. Of course, inviting Meg and Lindsey to the shop might have given Gary a clue. The idea of letting Lindsey see him at work had been an excuse; in reality

185

he'd been trying to impress Meg, show her how successful he was. Prove to her that he was worthy of her attention.

Steve had always kept his personal life separate from the business. His personal life — that was a joke. He'd worked for years, dedicating his life to building a thriving business. He'd been successful, but that success had come at a price. There was very little room in his life for love.

But there was room for Meg and Lindsey.

Meg's lithe body moved with the music provocatively, seductively, against his. He wanted to hold her even tighter, kiss her, caress her . . .

They stopped moving, the pretense of dancing more than he could sustain. "I want you so badly," he whispered.

Meg sighed and raised her head so their eyes met in the dim light. "I want you, too. It frightens me how much . . ."

He ran his fingers up through her hair and held his breath as he slowly lowered his mouth to hers. "Oh, Meg." He kissed her over and over, unable to get enough of her.

The sound of a throat being cleared suddenly penetrated his brain.

Lindsey. Again.

Steve groaned inwardly. Slowly, reluctantly, he loosened his grip on Meg and eased his body away from hers.

She resisted. "Don't stop."

"Lindsey's back," he whispered.

Meg buried her face in his sweater.

"Hello, again," Lindsey said cheerfully from the stairs. "It looks like I returned in the nick of time." She pranced down the steps, walked over to the wine bottle and sadly shook her head. "You didn't even open the wine."

"We didn't get a chance," Steve muttered.

"I gave you twenty minutes," she said. "From what I can see, that was about five minutes longer than I should've waited. You're a fast worker."

"Lindsey," Meg said, in what was obviously meant to be her sternest voice. Unfortunately, the effect was more tentative than severe.

"I know I'm making a pest of myself — and I apologize, I really do. But we've been talking about this stuff in my sex-ed. class, and there's a case to be made for abstinence."

"What's that got to do with your mother and me?" Steve made the mistake of asking.

"You don't really want me to answer that, do you?" Lindsey asked. "Mom's flustered enough as it is."

"I guess not."

"We could discuss safe sex, if you want."

Steve watched in fascination as Meg's face turned a deep shade of red. "Lindsey!" This time her mother's voice was loud and clear. "You're embarrassing me."

"Sorry, Mom, but I figured we should raise the subject now instead of later." She dropped down on the sofa, then reached for the wine bottle and examined the label. "It's a good month, too. September. Brenda's uncle bought it for us. He said it wasn't a great wine, but it'd get the job done."

Steve's hand gripped Meg's shoulder. "It was, uh, thoughtful of you."

"Thanks." She smiled broadly. "But we were going for the romantic element."

"Now," Steve said, "would you mind if your mother and I talked? By ourselves? We didn't get much of a chance to do that earlier."

"I suppose that'd be all right — only I need to know something first." She set the wine bottle down and looked intently at Steve. "Are you going to marry my mother?"

Meg made a small mewling noise that suggested she was mortified beyond words. She sank onto the ottoman and covered her face with both hands.

"Well, are you?" Lindsey pressed, ignoring her mother entirely.

Steve couldn't very well say he hadn't been thinking along those lines. There'd been little else on his mind for the past few days. He loved Meg. When he wasn't with her, it felt as if something was missing from his life. From his heart.

Steve had never imagined himself with a ready-made family, but he couldn't see himself without Meg and Lindsey. Not now.

"I believe that's a subject your mother and I need to discuss privately, but since you asked I'll tell you."

Lindsey got to her feet and Meg dropped her hands and looked up at him.

"You're going to marry us, aren't you." Lindsey's words were more statement than question. A satisfied smile lit up her face. "You're really going to do it."

"If your mother will have me."

"She will, trust me," Lindsey answered, looking gleeful. "I've known my mother forever and I've never seen her this gaga over a man."

"I can do my own talking, thank you very much," Meg said. "This is the most humiliating moment of my life — thanks to you, Lindsey Marie Remington." She stood, hands on her hips. "Go to your room and we'll talk when I've finished begging Steve to forgive you."

"What did I do that was so terrible?" Lindsey muttered.

Meg pointed to the stairs.

It looked as though Lindsey was about to argue; apparently she thought better of it. Her shoulders slumped forward and she moved slowly toward the stairs.

"I was just helping," she said under her breath.

"We'll talk about that later, young lady."

Lindsey's blue eyes met Steve's as she passed him. "I know I'm in trouble when she calls me *young lady.* She's mad. Be careful what you say. Don't ruin everything now."

"I'll try my best," Steve promised.

Meg waited until her daughter had reached the top of the stairs before she spoke. "I can't begin to tell you how sorry I am about that." Although her voice was calm, Steve wasn't fooled. Meg was angry, just as Lindsey had said.

"I'll have Lindsey apologize after I've had a chance to cool down," Meg was saying. "I don't dare speak to her now." She paced the carpet. "I want you to know I absolve you from everything that was said."

Steve rubbed his jaw. "Absolve me from what, precisely?"

"I want it understood, here and now, that

190

I don't expect you to marry me."

"But I like the idea."

"I don't," she flared. "Not when my daughter practically ordered you to propose. Now," she said with a deep breath, "I think it might be best if you left."

Steve tried to protest, but Meg ushered him to the door and he could see that this wasn't the time to reason with her.

"I've never been so mortified in my life," Meg told Laura. She counted the change and put it in the cash register. The store was due to open in ten minutes and she felt far from ready to deal with customers.

"But he said he wanted to marry you, didn't he?"

"It was a pity proposal. Good grief, what else could he say?"

Laura restocked the front display with the latest bestsellers. "Steve doesn't look like the kind of guy who'd propose if he didn't mean it."

"He didn't mean it."

"What makes you so sure?"

Meg wanted to find a hole, crawl inside and hide for the rest of her natural life. No one seemed to appreciate the extent of her humiliation. Steve certainly hadn't. He'd tried to conceal it from her, but he'd viewed the incident with Lindsey as one big joke.

She hadn't intended to mention it to anyone. Laura knew because she'd sensed something was wrong with Meg, and in a moment of weakness, Meg had blurted out the entire episode.

"Have you talked to Lindsey about what she did?" Laura asked.

"In my current frame of mind," Meg told her, "I thought it better not to try. I'll talk to her when I can do so without screaming or weeping in frustration."

"What I don't understand," Laura said, hugging a book to her chest, "is what happened to bring about such a reversal in her attitude to Steve. The last time we talked, you were pulling out your hair because she refused to believe he wasn't a convicted felon."

"I don't know what's going on with her. I just don't get it."

"You've got to admit, this romance between you and Steve has taken some unexpected twists and turns," Laura said. "First, you didn't even *want* to meet him, then once you did you agreed not to see each other again. It would've ended there if not for the flowers."

"Which didn't even come from Steve. He was just glad to be done with me."

"That's not the way I remember it."

"I doubt I'll ever see him again," Meg said, slamming the cash drawer shut.

"Now you're being ridiculous," Laura said.

"I wouldn't blame him. No man in his right mind would want to get tangled up with Lindsey and me."

"I'm sure that's not true."

Laura sounded so definite about that. Meg desperately wanted to believe her, but she knew better. When she closed the shop at six that evening, she still hadn't heard from Steve, which convinced Meg that he was relieved to be free of her.

Lindsey was sitting in the living room reading when Meg got home from work. "Hi," she said, taking a huge bite out of a big red Delicious apple.

Meg set aside her purse and slipped off her shoes. The tiles in the entryway felt cool against her aching feet.

"You're not mad at me anymore, are you?" Lindsey asked. She got off the sofa and moved into the kitchen, where Meg was pouring herself a glass of iced tea.

"You embarrassed me."

"Steve wasn't embarrassed," Lindsey said. "I don't understand why you're so upset."

"How would you feel if I called up Dale

Kotz and told him you wanted to go to the ninth-grade dance with him? He'd probably agree, because he likes you, but you'd never know if Dale would've asked you himself."

"Oh." Lindsey didn't say anything for several minutes.

"But it's more than that, Lindsey. I was mortified to the very marrow of my bones. I felt like you pressured Steve into proposing."

Lindsey sat in one of the kitchen chairs. "Would you believe me if I told you I was sorry?"

"Yes, but it doesn't change what happened."

"You are still angry, aren't you?"

"No," Meg said, opening the refrigerator and taking out lettuce for a salad. "I'm not angry anymore, just incredibly embarrassed and hurt."

"I didn't mean to hurt you, Mom," Lindsey said in a low voice. "I was only trying to help."

"I know, honey, but you didn't. You made everything much, much worse."

Lindsey hung her head. "I feel just awful."

Meg didn't feel much better herself. She sat down at the table, next to her daughter, and patted Lindsey's hand.

Lindsey managed a weak smile, then fell

into her mother's arms and hid her face against Meg's shoulder. "Men are so dumb sometimes," she murmured. "Brenda says love is like a game of connect the dots. Only with men, you have to make the dots and then draw the lines. They don't get it."

Meg stroked her daughter's hair.

"Do you love him, Mom?"

Meg smiled for the first time that day. "Yeah, I think I do. I certainly didn't plan on falling in love with him, that's for sure. It just sort of . . . happened."

"I don't think he expected to fall in love with you, either."

The doorbell chimed, and horrified that she might be caught crying, Lindsey broke away from her mother and hurriedly brushed the tears from her face.

"I'll get it," Meg said. She padded barefoot into the hallway and opened the door.

Steve stood on the other side, holding a dozen long-stemmed roses. He grinned. "Hello," he said, handing her the flowers. "I thought we'd try this marriage-proposal thing again, only this time we'll do it my way — not Lindsey's."

NINE

"Marriage proposal?" Meg repeated, staring down at the roses in her arms. "Really, Steve, there's no need to do this." Her throat was closing up on her; she could barely speak and she couldn't meet his eyes.

"I know exactly what I'm doing," Steve said.

"Is it Brenda?" Lindsey called from the kitchen.

"No, it's Steve."

"Steve!" Lindsey cried excitedly. "This is great. Maybe I didn't ruin everything after all."

"Hello, Meg," Steve said softly.

"Hi." She still couldn't look him in the eye.

"I'd like to talk to you."

"I . . . I was hoping we could do that," Meg told him. "They're lovely, thank you."

She handed Lindsey the flowers. "Would you take care of these for me?" she asked her daughter. "Steve and I are going to talk and we'd appreciate some privacy. Okay?"

"Sure, Mom."

Lindsey disappeared into the kitchen and Meg sat down on the sofa. Steve sat beside her and took her hand. She wished he wasn't so close. The man had a way of muddling her most organized thoughts.

"Before you say anything, I have a couple of things I'd like to talk to you about," she began. She freed her hand from his and clasped her knees. "I've been doing a lot of thinking and . . . and I've come to a few conclusions."

"About what?"

"Us," she said. Dragging in a deep breath, she continued. "Laura reminded me this afternoon that our relationship has taken some unexpected twists and turns. Neither one of us wanted to meet the other — we were thrown into an impossible situation.

"We wouldn't have seen each other again if it wasn't for the flowers your sister sent me. From the moment we met, we've had two other people dictating our lives."

"To some extent that's true," Steve agreed, "but we wouldn't have allowed any of this to happen if we hadn't been attracted to each other from the beginning."

"Maybe," she admitted slowly.

"What do you mean, maybe?" Steve asked.

"I think we both need some time apart to decide what we really want."

"No way!" he said. "I've had thirty-eight years to look for what I want and I've found it. I'd like to make you and Lindsey a permanent part of my life."

"Ah, yes. Lindsey," Meg said. "As you might have noticed, she's fifteen going on thirty. I have a feeling this is what the rest of the teen years are going to be like."

"So you could use a gentle hand to help you steer her in the right direction." Steve leapt to his feet and jerked his fingers through his hair. "Listen, if you're trying to suggest you'd rather not marry me, just say so."

Meg straightened, keeping her back stiff. For a moment she couldn't speak. "That's what I'm saying," she finally managed.

Steve froze, and it was clear to Meg that he was in shock. "I see," he said after a long pause. "Then what do you want from me?"

Meg closed her eyes. "Maybe it'd be best if we —"

"Don't say it, Meg," he warned in low tones, "because we'll both know it's a lie."

"Maybe it'd be best if we —" she felt she had to say the words "— didn't see each other for a while."

Steve's smile was filled with sarcasm. "Let me tell you something, Meg Remington, because someone obviously needs to. Your husband walked out on you and your daughter. It happens. It wasn't the first time a man deserted his family for another woman and it won't be the last. But you've spent the past ten years building a wall around you and Lindsey.

"No one else was allowed in until Lindsey took matters into her own hands. Now that I'm here, you don't know what to do. You started to care for me and now you're scared to death."

"Steve . . ."

"Your safe, secure world is being threatened by another man. Do you think I don't know you love me?" he demanded. "You're crazy about me. I feel the same way about you, and to be fair, you've done a damned good job of shaking up my world, too.

"If you want it to end here and now, okay, but at least be honest about it. You're pushing me away because you're afraid of knocking down those walls of yours. You're afraid to trust another man with your heart."

"You seem to have me all figured out," she said, trying — without much success — to sound sarcastic. To sound as if her emotions were unaffected by his words.

"You want me to leave without giving you this diamond burning a hole in my pocket, then fine. But don't think it's over, because it isn't. I don't give up that easily." He stalked out of the room and paused at her front door. "Don't get a false sense of security. I'll be back and next time I'm bringing reinforcements." The door closed with a bang.

"Mom," Lindsey asked, slipping into the room and sitting down next to Meg. "What happened?"

Meg struggled not to weep. "I . . . got cold feet."

"But you told me you were in love with Steve."

"I am," she whispered.

"Then why'd you send him away?"

Meg released her breath. "Because I'm an idiot."

"Then stop him," Lindsey said urgently.

"I can't. . . . It's too late."

"No, it isn't," Lindsey argued and rushed out the front door. A part of Meg wanted to stop her daughter. Meg's pride had taken enough of a beating in the past few days. But her heart, her treacherous heart, knew that the battle had already been lost. She was in love with Steve Conlan.

A minute later Lindsey burst into the

house, breathing hard. Panting, she said between giant gulps of air, "Steve says . . . if you want to talk to him . . . you're going to have to come outside . . . yourself."

Meg clasped her hands together. "Where is he?"

"Sitting in his truck. Hurry, Mom! I don't think . . . he'll wait much longer."

With her heart pounding, Meg walked onto the porch and leaned against the column. Steve's truck was parked at the curb.

He turned his head when he saw her. His eyes were cold. Unfriendly. Unwelcoming.

Meg bit her lip and met his gaze squarely. It took every ounce of resolve she had to move off the porch and take a few steps toward him. She paused halfway across the freshly mowed lawn.

Steve rolled down the window. "What?" he demanded.

She blinked, her heart racing.

"Lindsey said you had something you wanted to tell me," he muttered.

Meg should've known better than to let Lindsey do her talking for her. She opened her mouth, but her throat was clogged with tears. She tried to swallow, refusing to cry in front of him.

"Say it!"

"I . . . don't know if I can."

"Either you say it or I'm leaving." He turned away from her and started the engine.

"Mom, we're going to lose him," Lindsey cried from the porch. "Don't let him go. . . ."

"I . . . love you," she whispered.

Steve switched off the engine. "Did you say something?"

"I love you, Steve Conlan. I'm scared out of my wits. You're right — I have built a wall around us. I don't want to lose you. It's just that I'm . . . afraid." Her voice caught on the last word.

His eyes held hers and after a moment, he smiled. "That wasn't so difficult, now, was it?"

"Yes, it was," she countered. "It was incredibly hard." He didn't seem to realize she was standing on her front lawn with half the neighborhood looking on as she told him how much she loved him.

"You're going to marry me, Meg Remington."

She sniffled. "Probably."

He got out of his truck, slammed the door and with three long strides eliminated the distance between them. "Will you or will you not marry me?"

"I will," she said, laughing and crying at the same time, then she ran to meet him halfway.

"That's what I thought." Steve hauled her into his arms and buried her in his embrace. He grabbed her about the waist and whirled her around, then half carried her back into the house.

Once inside, he kicked the door shut and and they leaned against it, kissing frantically.

Lindsey cleared her throat behind them. "I hate to interrupt, but I have a few important questions."

Steve hid his face in Meg's neck and mumbled something she couldn't hear, which was no doubt for the best.

"Okay, kiddo, what do you want to know?" Steve asked when he'd regrouped.

"We're getting married?" Lindsey asked. Meg liked the way she'd included herself.

"Yup," Steve assured her. "We're going to be a family."

Lindsey let out a holler that could be heard three blocks away.

"Where will we live? Your house or ours?"

Steve looked at Meg. "Do you care?"

She shook her head.

"We'll live wherever you want," Steve told the girl. "I imagine staying close to your friends is important, so we'll take that into consideration."

"Great." Lindsey beamed him a smile. "What about adding to the family? Mom's willing, I think."

Once more Steve looked at Meg, and laughing, she nodded. "Oh, yes," she murmured, "there'll be several additions to this family."

Steve's eyes grew intense, and Meg knew he was thinking the same thing she was. She wanted his babies as much as she wanted this man. She loved him, desired him, anticipating all they could discover together, all they could learn from each other.

"One last thing," Lindsey said.

It was hard to pull her eyes away from Steve, but she wanted to include Lindsey in these important decisions. "Yes, honey?"

"It's just that I'd rather you didn't go shopping for your wedding dress alone. You're really good at lots of things, but frankly, Mom, you don't have any fashion sense."

As it turned out, Lindsey, Brenda and Steve's sister, Nancy, were all involved in the process of choosing the all-important wedding dress. Steve, naturally, wasn't allowed within a hundred feet of Meg and her dress until the day of the ceremony.

The wedding took place three months later, with family and friends gathered around. Lindsey proudly served as her mother's maid of honor.

Steve endured all the formality because he knew it mattered to Meg and to Lindsey. Nancy and his mother seemed to enjoy making plans for the wedding, too. All that was required of him was to show up and say "I do," which suited Steve just fine.

In his view, this fuss over weddings was for women. Men considered it a necessary evil. Or so he believed until his wedding day. When he saw Meg walk down the aisle, the emotion that throbbed in his chest came as a complete and utter surprise.

He'd known he loved her — he must, to put up with all the craziness that had befallen their courtship. But he hadn't realized how deep that love went. Not until he saw Meg so solemn and so beautiful. His bride. She stole his breath as he gazed at her.

The reception was a blur. Every time he looked at Meg he found it difficult to believe that this beautiful, vibrant woman was his wife. His thoughts were a jumbled, confused mess as he greeted those he needed to greet and thanked those he needed to thank.

It seemed half a lifetime before he was alone with his wife. He'd booked the honeymoon suite at a hotel close to Sea-Tac airport. The following morning they were flying to Hawaii for two weeks. Meg had never seen the islands. Steve suspected he didn't need a tropical playground to discover paradise. He would find that in her arms.

"My husband." Meg said the word shyly as Steve fumbled with the key card to unlock their suite. "I like the way it sounds."

"So do I, but not quite as much as I like the sound of wife." With the door open, he swept Meg into his arms and carried her into the room.

He hadn't taken two steps before they started to kiss.

Meg tasted of wedding cake and champagne, of passion and love. She wound her arms around his neck and enticed him to kiss her again. Steve didn't need much of an invitation.

At the unbridled desire he read in her eyes, Steve moaned and carried her to the bed. After he'd set her feet on the floor, he kissed her again, slowly, with all the pent-up desire inside him.

He reached behind her for the zipper of her dress. "I haven't made any secret of how much I want to make love to you."

"That's true," she whispered, kissing his jaw. "Thank you for agreeing to wait. It meant a lot to me to start our marriage this way."

He slipped the sleeve down her arm and kissed the ivory perfection of one shoulder. Then he kissed the other, his lips blazing a trail up the side of her neck to the hollow of her throat.

"You make my knees go weak," she told him in a low voice.

"Mine are, too."

Together they collapsed on the bed. Steve kissed her and loosened his tie. With their lips joined, Meg's fingers worked at his shirt, undressing him.

Soon they were lost in each other, loving each other, immersed in a world of their own. A world from which they didn't emerge until the summer sun had been replaced by a glittering moon and a sky full of stars.

Back at the reception, Lindsey sat with Steve's sister, Nancy, and licked the icing off their fingertips. "Do you suppose they'll ever figure it out?"

Nancy sipped champagne from a crystal flute. "I doubt either of them is thinking about much right now — except each other."

"We made some real mistakes, though."

"We?" Nancy said, eyeing Lindsey.

"Okay, me. I'll admit I nearly ruined everything by pushing the marriage issue. How was I to know my mother would take it so personally? Jeez, she just about had a heart attack, and all because I suggested Steve marry her."

"It worked out, though," Nancy said, looking pleased with herself. "And I made a few blunders of my own. Getting my friend to go to the shop and say she was Meg wasn't the smartest thing I've ever done. Steve was bound to find out sooner or later that it wasn't Meg."

"But we had to do something," Lindsey insisted. "They were both being so stubborn. One of them had to give in. Besides, your ploy worked."

"Better than the flowers I sent."

Lindsey sampled another bite of wedding cake. "You know what was the hardest part?"

"I know what it was for me. I had one heck of a time keeping a straight face when your mother came to the house dressed in a Tina Turner wig and five-inch heels. Oh, Lindsey, if you could've seen her."

"Steve was pretty funny himself, with his leather jacket and that bad-boy smirk."

"Neither one of them's any good at acting," Nancy said, still grinning.

"Not like us."

"Not like us," Nancy agreed.

ABOUT THE AUTHOR

Debbie Macomber is a number one *New York Times* bestselling author. Her recent books include *92 Pacific Boulevard, 8 Sandpiper Way, 74 Seaside Avenue* and *Debbie Macomber's Cedar Cove Cookbook* as well as *Twenty Wishes, A Cedar Cove Christmas, Summer on Blossom Street* and *The Perfect Christmas.* She has become a leading voice in women's fiction worldwide and her work has appeared on every major bestseller list, including those of the *New York Times, USA TODAY, Publishers Weekly* and *Entertainment Weekly.* She is a multiple award winner, and she won the 2005 Quill Award for Best Romance. There are more than 100 million copies of her books in print. For more information on Debbie and her books, visit her Web site, www.DebbieMacomber.com.

We hope you have enjoyed this Large Print book. Other Thorndike, Wheeler, Kennebec, and Chivers Press Large Print books are available at your library or directly from the publishers.

For information about current and upcoming titles, please call or write, without obligation, to:

Publisher
Thorndike Press
295 Kennedy Memorial Drive
Waterville, ME 04901
Tel. (800) 223-1244

or visit our Web site at:

http://gale.cengage.com/thorndike

OR

Chivers Large Print
published by AudioGO Ltd
St James House, The Square
Lower Bristol Road
Bath BA2 3SB
England
Tel. +44(0) 800 136919
www.audiogo.co.uk

All our Large Print titles are designed for easy reading, and all our books are made to last.